THE
SWEET
DEAD LIFE

THE
SWEET
DEAD LIFE

JOY PREBLE

Published in the United States in 2013 by Soho Teen
an imprint of
Soho Press, Inc.
853 Broadway
New York, NY 10003

Library of Congress Cataloging-in-Publication Data
Preble, Joy.
The sweet dead life / Joy Preble.
p. cm.
ISBN 978-1-61695-150-4
eISBN978-1-61695-151-1
1. Mystery and detective stories. 2. Angel—Fiction. 3. Dead—Fiction.
4. Brothers and sisters—Fiction. 5. Missing persons—Fiction. I. Title.
PZ7.P90518Sw 2013
[Fic]—dc23   2012033352

Interior design by Janine Agro, Soho Press, Inc.

Printed in the United States of America

10 9 8 7 6 5 4 3 2 1

For Jake—who finds the universe as strange and wonderful and darkly amusing as I do.

"You may all go to hell and I will go to Texas."
—Davy Crockett

THE
SWEET
DEAD LIFE

I found out two things today: One, I think I'm dying. And two, my brother is a perv.

My friend Maggie says that things happen for a reason. This is how Mags thinks: that there's an explanation for everything. Like the time in second grade when I got the flu and couldn't go on the class trip to Huntsville to see the giant statue of Sam Houston. Maggie says the universe spit this out on purpose. If I'd been there, maybe something bad would have happened, like a pigeon crapping in my hair while I stared up at Sam's enormous head. Or someone might have broken into our house, but didn't because he peeked through the window and saw me lying on the couch all feverish, watching the *Price is Right*. Maggie believes the world works like that.

Me? I don't. This drives Mags nuts, but like my dad used to say, "You believe what you believe. Who am I to say you're batshit crazy?"

My father bailed on us when I was nine and we haven't

seen him since, but at least he left me words to live by and a colorful vocabulary. Unfortunately, the administration of Ima Hogg Junior High is not a fan of colorful vocabulary. Even though I'm probably dying of some strange disease— I'll get to that in a second—they had no problem assigning me three days of after-school detention, otherwise known as ASD, for calling my algebra teacher Mr. Collins an asshat. Which he is.

You would think a school named after a woman whose parents had an obvious screw loose in the naming department would be more reasonable. You would think.

So this is what I was going to tell Casey—a.k.a. my perv brother—when I walked into his room: that he had to give me a ride for the next three afternoons because the state of Texas had cut the budget, meaning there was no more late bus for juvenile offenders like me, and it was too far to walk in my currently dying condition.

True, at that moment, I didn't know for sure I was dying. The doctors have been shifty about actually telling me there's no cure for what I have. I'm just a fourteen-year-old girl who had to quit track because I can't run even as far as the mailbox anymore without gasping for breath. I've got weird rashes on my feet and funny dark patches on my tongue. My white blood cell count is out of whack. I'm always cold and I'm thirsty even though I drink like a camel preparing for a desert trip. And just for grins, my pee has started looking a mite green.

Here's what I don't have: Cancer. Diabetes. Scabies. Ebola. Meningitis. Beri beri. Flu. Congestive Heart Failure. Pica. Exploding Head Syndrome. (Yes, it's real. Look it up!)

Anyway, Casey's silver Prius was in the driveway this afternoon when I got home. It's really my mom's car, but

Mom isn't exactly driving much these days. She's not paying the bills much either, but that's another story. And here's the thing I've learned about a Prius. If your stoner brother (yes, Casey the perv) leaves it running all night because, in his words, "It's like a stealth-mobile. Really, Jenna, I had no idea it was on," it likely will *not* be able to take either of you to school the next morning. And if your brother lets his stoner pal Dave borrow it to go get tacos at Jack in the Box at 2 A.M., it's likely to come back with the hood scratched and a huge dent in the front bumper. Not to mention likely stinking of a combination of grease and weed.

"Likely" is a word I toss around a lot when it comes to Casey, because even when he tells the truth—which, in fact, he usually does—he still sounds like the worst liar ever.

Dave blamed the accident on the Prius dash display. According to Dave, it's extremely distracting because you can set it to show when the car is running on battery. The blinking lights freaked him out, causing him to close his eyes after placing his taco order. This is why he bashed into the drive-through menu. In no way did Dave believe that this incident related to what he had inhaled prior to the taco run.

Dave to Jack in the Box worker: Dude. I'm stuck in the menu.

Jack: Dos tacos. That's Spanish for dos tacos.

I walked in, tossed my backpack on the couch and headed upstairs. Mom's door was closed. No surprise there. I thought about knocking. The thought didn't last long. I could hear whatever was on her TV, a cooking show by the sound of it. Mom hasn't cooked a meal in at least a year, but she's got this thing for the Food Network. "That Paula Deen," she commented the other day, "do you know she used to be afraid to leave the house? Now look at her."

I didn't want to look at Paula Deen. I wanted my mother to snap out of whatever kept *her* inside most of the day. I mean, look at *me*. My pee had begun looking like a vat of dye for green Life Savers. But when your mother spends the day in the same sweats and T-shirt in which she's spent the last three days and nights, telling her that maybe you've got some freaky jungle fever probably isn't going to make a difference.

Last week, I proved this theory by showing her my tongue. It was covered with dots. She cried and told Casey to take me to the dentist. Then cried some more when we reported that: a) The Visa card was rejected and we now owed the dentist $250 and b) Dr. Kensington had informed me that the tongue was "mysterious."

I climbed the stairs, tired and pissed at Mr. Collins and the Ima Hogg detention policy. My boots felt too heavy for my legs, which was a definite bummer because I loved those boots. They were red square-toed Ariats that I'd gotten at Bubba's Boot Town. I still had the receipt—not because I planned on returning them, but because it listed the name of the guy who'd sold them to me. I was wearing boots that had been fitted by a salesman sporting a huge Texas-shaped silver belt buckle, whose name tag identified him as Jesus. You don't return boots like that, even if some weird disease is making it hard for you to walk in them.

Casey's door was closed. I knocked. It was probably hard for him to hear me over the sound of Katy Perry singing about wanting to see someone's peacock. So I turned the knob and walked in.

My brother was slouched against the headboard of his bed, his laptop on the comforter and his right hand down his jeans. He was wearing a Mountain Dew T-shirt with a stain on the front. He was breathing sort of heavily. The state of

Texas did not believe in sex education, but we still had cable and high-speed Internet. I was not unaware of what he was doing.

"Gross," I hollered. It took Casey a few seconds to register my presence. He scowled and yanked his hand out of his pants. If there is anything worse than being saddled with an unidentifiable disease and three days of detention, it is walking into your brother's room to find him, unzipped, on a porn site. Correction: I had no idea if he was looking at porn since I couldn't see the laptop screen. For all I knew, he was looking at pictures of the Grand Canyon. Which might explain his lack of a girlfriend.

Actually, what explained his lack of a girlfriend is that he still hadn't recovered from Lanie Phelps, his first and only love who broke his heart sophomore year by dumping him for (among other things) being the kind of guy who gets stoned alone, and, well, you get the picture. Lanie was blonde. Lanie was a cheerleader. Lanie was the walking cliché who, according to Casey, had informed him that the breakup wasn't because he quit football. It was because he stopped "walking proud," and she was having a hard time with that.

Of course, he didn't tell her the truth: that he quit football to help save our bank account.

A pain sliced through my head. It hurt so hard that I gasped. Tiny white dots hazed my vision. Terrific. My brother is pleasuring himself to pictures of the Colorado River and I'm the one who's going blind. I clutched at my temples. Katy Perry was now reminiscing about the taste of cherry Chap-Stick. The smell of stale marijuana and possibly the remains of a tuna sandwich wafted through my nostrils. I crumpled slowly to the floor. I'd have fallen faster, but the Ariats made my legs less flexible. Thank you, Jesus.

I hit the carpet with a thud and my cheek pressed against something squishy that I was too distracted to identify. Above me on the bed, I heard Casey holler. It sounded like "Jenna, don't break my bong." Or maybe, "Jenna, I'm going to sing a song."

"I think I'm going to puke," I managed. Could heads actually split in two like in a cartoon? Because that's what mine felt like it was doing.

"Hang on," he said. I felt more than saw him fling himself off the bed. "Lemme get the garbage can."

I lay on Casey's less-than-clean cream carpet, taking shallow breaths and trying not to vomit. The room was silent. Maybe Casey had turned down the volume. Or else I was going deaf along with everything else. I willed myself not to pass out and—since I had nothing better to do—scanned the crap under Casey's bed, which seemed to include a lot of wadded up pieces of Kleenex. A plate with half of what was definitely that tuna sandwich I'd smelled was sitting in the middle of the used tissues.

Note to self: Spray laptop with Lysol before using.

"Here." Casey shoved the garbage can at my head. "Can you sit up?"

"Only if your pants are zipped."

"Ha ha. Did you ever hear of knocking?"

"I have three days of after-school detention," I said, because honestly this was why I came in here, wasn't it?

I managed to ease myself off the floor. Casey kneeled next to me holding the garbage can like he was offering me a prize. His hair was sticking up at funny angles. His breath smelled like corn nuts. His eyes looked red. He reached up and picked what turned out to be a half-chewed corn nut off my cheek. Then he smoothed my hair back and held it while I vomited into the can.

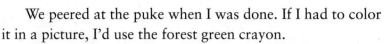

We peered at the puke when I was done. If I had to color it in a picture, I'd use the forest green crayon.

"What have you been eating?" Casey asked. He stared at the puke some more and then at me. I wiped a stray dot of vomit off my Ariats. I had recently cleaned them with the leather conditioner that Jesus had talked me into along with the boots.

"Nothing. Nauseous all day. Oh wait—I had an apple slice during nutrition." Nutrition was what Ima Hogg called our fifteen-minute break. I guess because we were too old for them to call it recess.

"Oh."

"Yeah," I said. "Take your hand off my head. I know where it's been."

Then I passed out.

When I came to, we both agreed that maybe I was dying.

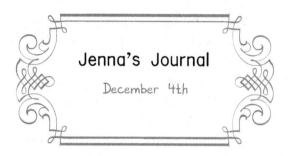

Jenna's Journal

December 4th

SPRING CREEK HIGH SCHOOL
Casey Samuels Progress Report
Calculus: 52
Honors US History: 12
AP English: 67
Teen Leadership: 33
AP Chemistry: 70
European History: 0

We dealt with my (maybe—possibly? yes . . . it might be the truth) dying condition the way we dealt with everything these days: we hoped it would go away. This isn't exactly an action-filled activity. I told Casey I would be all right—or at least no worse than I already was—and that he needed to get back in the semi-wrecked Prius and drive on an angle to work. I thought about telling him to keep his hands out of his pants while he was on the road, but I figured he had learned his lesson by having his sister faint dead away in his room after catching him in the act.

Okay, we both knew that wasn't why I passed out. But if it could put a stop to my brother's self-love, I was all for it.

"I'll bring you back something," he said as he helped me to my room. "I'll take care of Mom, too," he added. "You just rest. Or do your homework or something."

The fainting and the puking had suddenly made me hungry. Or at least now the slightly nauseous feeling I'd had all day was gone and I was aware that maybe I should eat.

"Brisket sandwich," I said. "And French fries. But only if Jorge is working the fryer." Jorge Garcia was a genius at making French fries. He was about five foot four and from Guatemala and the best line cook at BJ's BBQ, where my brother waited tables four nights a week. Casey'd gotten the job through Dave before Dave was fired for toking up in the back.

True story: Casey's name tag at BJ's doesn't say Casey. It says Dick. When I noticed this and asked him about it here's what he said: *"This way I can say to customers, 'Welcome to BJ's. I'm Dick.'"*

This, ladies and gentlemen, is the boy who shares my gene pool.

As he left my room, a piece of paper fluttered out of the back pocket of his jeans and landed on the floor. I started to yell after him, then saw the words Spring Creek High School and shut my mouth.

I waited until he pounded downstairs, then plucked his progress report off the floor, and climbed into bed. I loved my bed. It was a queen-size my parents had bought me right before our family situation went screwy. Luckily they'd popped for a goose-down duvet and brown and white cover

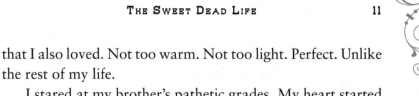

that I also loved. Not too warm. Not too light. Perfect. Unlike the rest of my life.

I stared at my brother's pathetic grades. My heart started throbbing like it had before I passed out, but not because I was about to faint again. I blinked a few times. If Mr. Collins saw me right now, I know what he'd say. *"Jenna Samuels. What's up with the crying? Your brother was the best running back Ima Hogg ever had. But he's a quitter. I put my rear on the line for that boy, talked him up to all the Spring Creek coaches. And what does the little pissant do? Up and quits the football team sophomore year. So think twice about wanting to follow in his footsteps, young lady."*

I know this because it's exactly what he said to me while waving my less-than-completed homework in my face. Somehow my lack of desire to slog through five pages of algebra problems made me a slacker. That I already had an A in Algebra—and that Mr. Collins was a shitty teacher who preferred worksheets to actual teaching—didn't seem to weigh into his thought process. Instead, he simultaneously called me out and dissed my brother. Calling him an asshat was a logical response.

But somehow I was the one with three days of ASD. Go figure.

Here's the conversation we didn't have:

"Hey Asshat Collins, you know what? Casey quit football because he's working two jobs. Casey's working two jobs because we have no health insurance and the five doctors who haven't been able to figure out what's wrong with me still want to be paid. Mom hasn't had a paycheck in over a year. Her savings account—which turns out had been sizeable from sources unknown—is currently down to $875.53, a sum that is less than our mortgage payment. Which hasn't

been paid in five months. Oh: And on the nights that Casey isn't at BJ's serving brisket and ribs and recommending the blackberry cobbler with vanilla ice cream, which by the way I used to love before everything began to taste more or less like sawdust, he delivers Chinese food for Beijing Bistro. Our Prius reeks of egg rolls and sweet and sour pork in addition to the weed odor and the grease from Dave's taco habit. So if you and the wife and three little Collins rugrats feel like moo shu this weekend, you know who to call. Don't forget to tip."

I wiped my eyes with the back of my hand.

The throwing up and the almost crying had made me dehydrated. Slowly, I eased out of bed. When I was sure I wasn't going to crash to the floor, I shuffled downstairs to the kitchen. Even in my condition I was not about to drink bathroom water.

At the sink, I chugged two glasses—so thirsty!—then found a container of orange juice in the fridge with a semi-respectable expiration date. I gulped from the carton, and emptied the rest into my glass. We might be broke, but I was still a manners girl.

I exited the kitchen with my juice at the same exact moment Mom stepped out of her room. As usual, she was wearing an ancient pair of red sweats from Victoria's Secret that were way too big and a pink Cockrell Butterfly Exhibit T-shirt I'd gotten at the Science and History Museum when I was nine, about a month before Dad decided that he wanted to be elsewhere. I'd put it in a bag of clothes to give away but somehow it had ended up in her wardrobe. Possibly because it fit her. Her hair was greasy and pulled back into a ponytail, but she'd swiped on some blush and eye shadow and lip gloss like she was trying to make an effort, which was definitely not something she'd been doing lately.

I stared at her.

She stared back.

"Did you take your vitamin today?" I asked her.

I was so tired I couldn't remember if I'd handed her one this morning, which I usually did. Her old boss, Dr. Stuart Renfroe, had given us a bunch of free sample bottles, for which I was grateful. (Mom used to be a speech therapist at Oak View Convalescent before she became a convalescent herself and stopped leaving the house.) Some days, it was the only sure nutrition that crossed her lips. Usually she was willing to swallow one every day. Unlike when Casey had recently suggested that maybe she should ask her boss for her old job back.

"Dr. Renfroe cares about you," Casey had told her. "He'd give you a few hours. I know he would." But Mom had just gotten teary and stiff-looking.

"Casey's gonna bring you something to eat later," I said, thinking it a better conversation starter than: *Hey, I'm puking green now.* "Maybe that salad. You know, the one with the chopped meat and eggs and stuff?"

She nodded. Her eyes looked watery. She had managed the eye shadow but not mascara and her eyelashes looked almost non-existent.

"I was thirsty," I added when she didn't respond. "You want something to drink?" I gestured with my shoulder to the kitchen in case she needed a context clue.

"I'm fine," my mother said.

I rocked on the heels of my Ariats, took a long drink of my remaining juice, and told myself to stay calm. I hate being lied to about as much as I hate being judged by people like Mr. Collins who think they know all there is to know about me because of my brother. (Although Casey had tidied himself up and changed out of his Mountain Dew shirt into his much dressier *Chicks Dig Nerds* shirt before he left for work.) *Note to self: Casey and I need to have a conversation about the very clear—to me—connection between his fashion sense and his lack of female attention.*

My mother was absolutely not fine. The Samuels family was absolutely not fine. "Really, Mom?"

She was silent. I didn't want her to be. Then she opened her mouth. "Your father . . ." she began.

I blinked at her, hard. "What about him?"

"I've been calling around," she said. "I've been online. Maybe I think I saw something about him there . . . ?"

I nearly dropped the glass. "Maybe?" *What the*—Calling around? Online? Was she serious? She hadn't mentioned Dad in months, and now, all of a sudden she's searching for him again? "What are you talking about?" I demanded.

"Jenna," Mom said, fingers knotting around the monarch butterfly in the middle of her T-shirt like she was trying to squash it. "There's stuff you don't know."

"What stuff? Dad stuff? Other stuff?"

I think she started to answer. Her mouth was moving again and I think she was forming words.

"Mom," I said. "Mom." The glass dropped from my hand, shattering on the hardwood floor. Sticky juice splattered my ankles. I could see but not hear that my mother was screaming. I started to shake. I was so cold. Unbelievably freezing. What the hell was wrong with me?

"Mommy," I whispered. My knees buckled. Even my boots weren't enough to stop it this time. Everything went black.

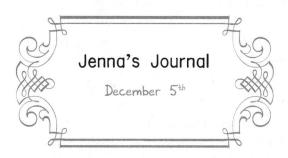

Jenna's Journal

December 5th

The way my brother tells it, he had just served a family-sized platter of peach cobbler with Blue Bell French Vanilla ice cream when Bryce, BJ's assistant manager, hurried over from the front register.

In case anyone is interested, Bryce isn't exactly in the running for World's Most Desirable Bachelor. He's about thirty (although it's hard to tell), maybe 250 pounds (again hard to tell), lives in a doublewide trailer on his parents' property in the back of Château Hills—a subdivision that absolutely does not contain French mansions—and collects comic books. Bryce is the kind of guy stores like Spencer's are made for. If you ever walked by Spencer's at the mall and wondered, hey, who spends eighty bucks on a six-foot beer pong table or twenty bucks on The Fartinator, Bryce is your answer. Well, so is Casey, actually. But that's not the point here.

The point is that Bryce skid to a lumbering stop in front of the vat of cobbler, gave it a brief but longing glance, and then told Casey that his mother was on the phone. As Casey tells it, Bryce insisted that Casey leave immediately, and that Bryce would cover for him, but only just this once.

I guess my having some sort of potentially fatal seizure just as my mother was about to impart the secret of the century (not that Bryce or Casey knew this) was only good enough for a one-night reprieve from BJ's. Which is handy to know if I make it to sixteen and am in need of part-time employment.

After that, things got a little crazy. Even for us.

Normally, I don't write stuff down that I haven't seen with my own eyes, but as mine were mostly rolled to the back of my head, I'm going to have to believe Casey's version of what came next. And as no one would really believe it anyway, it's the best I can do.

So. According to Casey, he ran to the Prius and headed home. I was still shaking and seizing. It's not like I could have told him that Mom had just admitted that maybe she knew where Dad was. Even if I could, it's not like he would have stopped to listen.

What he did know was that maybe I hadn't kept my promise about not dying while he was at work—and that bills or no bills, money or no money, he had to get me to the hospital. My mother had conveniently freaked out again. Very helpful, per usual. She was crying and screaming and rocking back and forth in a way that was not exactly compatible with squeezing into the back of our beat-up but environmentally friendly vehicle. So when we hit the road toward Houston Memorial Hospital Northside, it was just me and my brother and a car that drove like a drunk who couldn't walk a straight line.

"Stay with me, Jenna," Casey said as if quoting dialogue from some sappy Lifetime movie. He reached over and patted

me on the shoulder. The Prius angled right, bouncing over those speed bump thingies and onto the shoulder. Casey yanked the wheel. We barreled back into our lane. I had nothing left inside me to puke up, so I dry-heaved a couple of times instead. The lingering aroma of Dave's tacos wasn't helping.

"Not going anywhere," I croaked. *Unless you bash us into the guardrail. Then all bets are off.*

Casey grunted. I checked my seatbelt. The hospital exit was about half a mile away. My vision was going all wonky. Everything was covered in a cloudy haze. I was freezing again—so cold that my teeth started knocking against each other like a bunch of crazed woodpeckers.

"Casey." My voice was so tiny I could barely hear myself. "I don't think I'm going to make it."

Through the haze, I looked down at my Ariats. I wondered if maybe I should pipe up and tell him that I wanted to be buried in them. No sense letting Goodwill have my favorite boots. Not that I'm opposed to charitable contributions. But I loved my Ariats. If I was headed to the afterlife, at least I could go in style. I felt certain that Jesus would agree. Especially since he'd made an extra commission from that leather cleaner. I took one last lingering look at my boots and tried not to dry heave again. Then I blacked out.

Casey says that we made it to our exit. Apparently we were racing along the feeder road to the hospital about a mile down. (Just to paint the full picture: we passed Wood-haven Cemetery, Houston North Rehab, and a strip center that housed a spinal surgery facility with a prosthesis clinic attached, a Vietnamese noodle house, Café Monterrey Mexican restaurant, and Stacy Carrigan Legal. In the Texas suburbs we like to cover all bases. If the ER or the rehab couldn't fix you, at least they didn't have to cart you far. After that, your loved ones could get a bite to eat and chat about who they could sue.)

"We're almost there," I heard Casey say as I lurched into consciousness again.

And then we drifted to the right. I stared out the window in curious detachment as we clipped the side of a Ford F250 Super Cab coming out of the strip center, lifted into the air, and smacked down into the ditch on the side of the road. Then we began to tumble. Priuses are stout little things. They do not tumble well.

"Shit!" my brother yelled. He slammed his arm into my stomach like this might keep me from hitting the windshield. "Jenna!"

It felt like we flipped for hours. My air bag released. I know this because it smacked me in the chest. Somehow we'd gone airborne again during the tumbling. I was too dizzy to do anything but squeeze my eyes shut. When I opened them, we were right-side-up in the parking lot, Pho Fun Noodles to our right. Everything in my body felt like it had been smashed or set on fire or both. My left eye felt swollen. With enormous effort, I turned my head.

In the driver's seat, my brother was very, very still. His *Chicks Dig Nerds* T-shirt was covered in blood. So was his face, his hair, his neck. A huge dark gash cut down his cheek. More blood.

My air bag was smashed against me, its plasticky burning smell assaulting my nostrils. Weren't air bags supposed to deflate once they'd done their job?

Casey's air bag had not deployed.

"Casey!" I screamed, at least in my head. "Casey!"

Why wasn't he moving? Why wasn't he talking? Why

hadn't the damn air bag done what it was supposed to do? Because Dave had screwed up our car, that's why. Damn Dave and his marijuana habit and his taco obsession and his inability to drive. Except that wasn't all of it. This was my Mom's car. If she'd been driving it rather than hiding in the house from something that didn't even make sense, then maybe none of this would have happened. Normal Mom wouldn't have let us loan our car to Dave.

I have never seen a dead person before except on TV. My expectation had been that the first dead person I would actually encounter would be me. Because that was the other reason this had happened. My brother was driving *me* to the hospital. And now he wasn't breathing.

Somewhere in the distance I heard a siren. The air bag was pinning me to my seat and I was still hollering Casey's name. I was so weak and so tired and I couldn't even cry.

"You can't be dead," I whispered, my mouth moving against the stinky air bag. "You just can't be dead. I haven't even told you what Mom said. And if you're dead there won't be anyone to pick me up from after-school detention."

Casey didn't answer.

The siren wailed louder. *Ambulance*, I thought.

My airway was still being cut off by the huge white bag, but I felt a single tear drip from my swollen eye. I was dying of causes unknown, and my brother looked . . . If I hadn't passed out again, I probably would have gotten hysterical.

A bright light roused me. The ambulance was here. Probably a fire truck, too. Somewhere, I heard music. Instrumental, maybe? Mostly drumming. What kind of ER driver cranks the radio? Maybe they'd sent a helicopter. Why were there searchlights? It seemed awfully bright for a searchlight.

Had my eyes been hurt in the accident? I had enough wrong with me already.

I tried to pull my arm from under the air bag, but I couldn't. Maybe I had dislocated my shoulder. The brightness of the ambulance light kept pressing right through my eyelids.

"Casey?" I forced my eyes open, squinting in a strange flickering strobe light. It was like last Christmas when our next-door neighbors, the Gilroys, screwed in so many multi-colored bulbs that they blew the power grid to our cul-de-sac. Their gigantic blow-up Santa had deflated and bent over like an arthritic senior citizen. "Casey?" I managed again.

Blink. I saw Casey, illuminated in the glare. *Blink.* He still wasn't moving. *Blink.* He was still covered in blood. *Oh God. Help me. Please. Don't let Casey be dead. And while you're at it—if you're listening—don't let me die, either. I didn't want to be the girl who flipped over in a beat-up Prius that stunk of stale cannabis and then died of scabies.*

I knew I didn't have scabies, by the way. But this was a crisis. I needed to call it something.

There was a rushing sound and then something flapping. Was the helicopter going to land on the damn car?

The light strobed some more—so crazily now that it looked like that last blast of fireworks on the Fourth of July, that moment they send up everything they've got and the whole sky is filled with popping sounds and sparklers and trails of smoke and you've got this smile on your face a mile wide because it's just that amazing.

"Jenna." I thought I heard my brother. "Jenna . . ."

The bright light blinked out, and so did I.

Jenna's Journal

December 5th
LATER

"Jenna!"

A vaguely familiar man's voice echoed somewhere near my forehead. The bright light was still there. I could feel it through my eyelids. A whoosh of warm, minty breath rushed up my nostrils. I wiggled my toes. Someone had taken off my boots.

"Jenna," the voice said, "I need you to open your eyes." The mint breath swirled into my nose again. Whoever he was, he had impeccable dental hygiene.

With effort—they felt sticky and gluey and like they were filled with sand—I pried open my eyes. In the fuzziness, all I could make out was a tuft of curly black chest hair poking out from the V of green scrubs. Oh, and very white teeth.

"You're a lucky girl," he said as I squinted at him. Someone needed to turn down those lights. Was I dead after all? Was he the greeting committee? Did he know that he could wax that chest hair?

"Lucky?" My voice sounded like a rusty hinge. I wished he'd turn that damn light off. Why was my head so foggy?

"You've been in a car accident, Jenna. Do you remember?"

Shit. I sat up. Every inch of my body hollered that this was the wrong thing to do. A pinch of pain shot through my hand. I looked down. An IV was pumping something into my veins. A female voice squawked a code number over the PA system. A cart with various instruments and a couple of bloody cloths sat to my right. An ugly striped curtain rippled as someone walked by outside my little cubicle.

"You're in the ER, Jenna. At Houston Northside. I'm Dr. Renfroe. Remember?"

Dr. Renfroe? Mom's former boss at Oak View Convalescent? Aside from Bryce in a fit of kindness, he was the only one who seemed to give a crap about our family these days. But he didn't belong here. Maybe I was seeing things. Maybe I had a head injury. And where was . . .

"Casey?" I gasped. "Where's Casey?"

I looked around wildly. Where the hell was my brother? What had happened back there in the car? All that flipping. Casey, lying so still. All that blood. And light. There'd been an eyeball-searing strobe. And the air bag that hadn't—

"He's right outside, Jenna." Doctor Chest Hair smiled. "Now that you're awake, I'm sure he's dying to see you."

Dying to see me? So I wasn't hallucinating. Only Dr. Stuart Renfroe made jokes like that. (*"Jenna,"* he'd said the first time I met him, *"When's a door not a door? When it's ajar."*) The chest hair had thrown me, that's all. Until this moment I'd always seen him in a suit and tie. Just like Dr. Renfroe to say "dying to see" while I was sprawled in an ER cubicle possibly still expiring from not-scabies and hollering for my

brother. My brain flashed to Casey's face again, to that huge gash on his cheek.

Another wave of panic washed over me. What was Dr. Renfroe doing in the ER anyway, in scrubs? Maybe he was lying to me about Casey. Maybe they'd called him in to tell me the bad news. I wanted Casey to be okay, but how could Casey be okay?

"Are you," I began. "Why are you—"

"I work here a couple evenings a week," Dr. Renfroe said. "My little gift to the community."

Whatever. "Casey!"

The curtain swiped open. My brother walked in.

Okay. Pause here. Deep breaths. It's hard to describe how wonderful he looked. Seriously, the cliché is true. Words can't do this particular image justice.

Sure, there were some stray flecks of dried blood on his cheeks, but compared to how he'd looked in the car—his face smeared—he was pretty cleaned up. Also, his eyes looked better: no purple sacks underneath, none of the usual redness. They were bone white and sort of sparkly. Even in my weakened condition, I knew this was weird. Not only had we been in a car wreck, but let's face it: My brother smoked a lot of weed. His eyes hadn't been clear in months. Plus there was his posture. As he loped toward me, he looked somehow taller. Or at least not so slouchy. Maybe you stand up a little when you know you haven't bitten the dust on your sister's behalf.

"I could hear you all the way out in the waiting room," he said. He leaned over and gave me a gentle hug.

"You're not dead," I choked out. I didn't want to blubber in front of him, but I was close.

I had no idea how this was possible. But hell, I was all

for it. I was alive. Casey was alive. Doctor Chest Hair Renfroe was alive. It was all good things here in the ER. I knew I probably still had not-Ebola. And even *that* wasn't acting up right now.

"Nope, I'm fine," Casey said. "Doc Renfroe made me wait until you were awake."

He stopped hugging me and straightened. There was an odd look on his face, something beyond: *Hey I'm really sorry I almost killed you because I forgot to adjust for stoner-induced Prius drift.* Had I only imagined that deep cut on his cheek? I *must have* hit my head during the accident.

"What happened?" I managed in a rasp. "How come you smell so nice?" My brother smelled of something I couldn't quite place: something way better than his usual combo of cheap cologne from CVS Pharmacy, barbeque sauce, stale egg rolls and pot.

"I do?" Casey's brows shot up.

"Yeah. And why—"

"I called a taxi cab for Mom," he interrupted. "She's on her way."

I tried to give him the stink eye for changing the subject, but my face hurt too much to scrunch it up like that. "Since when do you know how to call a cab?" (Let me note for the record that taxis are rare in the Houston suburbs: like finding endangered whooping cranes or something. Maggie called one about a year ago when we wanted to go shopping at the Galleria and her mom refused to take us. The guy showed up in a raggedy SUV with peeling paint and told us it would be fifty bucks each way. His name was Wayne and he had an artificial right leg. We decided to shop local.)

"Cause we're minors. Cause if I want to get you out of here, she has to sign the release papers."

Oh. Okay. What wasn't okay: my brother sounded like a responsible human being. Mom's catatonic depression had clearly taken its toll on him. My heart flopped in my chest. Maybe I *was* dying. Casey was just doing his best for my last hurrah.

"I told her you're doing all right," Casey continued. "She seemed out of it again."

This didn't surprise me. Still, there was that bombshell before I passed out and she called Casey at work. Now she probably didn't even remember what she'd said about Dad. Maybe she'd made it all up, that stuff about keeping things secret. I guess we'd know soon enough.

"How is your mother?" Renfroe asked. He tapped at my IV bag, then scribbled something on a clipboard.

"Same," Casey said. He gave my hand a squeeze.

Not even Dr. Renfroe knew how much Mom had deteriorated. If he had, he might be sending over more than just free vitamin samples. Maybe something like Child Protective Services. Definitely not what we needed.

The ugly striped curtain parted again. Another guy in green scrubs, with a stethoscope around his neck joined us. He was quickly followed by a twenty-something woman in navy cargo pants with a tucked-in short-sleeved blue collared shirt, and what looked like a utility belt.

"Hey Amber," Casey said to the woman, as if he knew her.

Amber. I repeated the name to myself. Granted, my head was still pounding like a construction site. But *I* didn't know her. Who was Amber? And why was she smiling at my brother like she a) knew him and b) found him likeable?

"I'm Amber Velasco," she said, as if that explained everything. She tightened the elastic on her thick brown ponytail and smoothed her already smooth bangs. Her dark blue eyes roved over me. "I'm one of the EMTs who pulled you from the wreck. You had us scared there, Jenna." She shot a look at Casey.

He nodded.

My head gave another throb. Something about the way this Amber chick and Casey made eye contact reminded me of the kind of glances he and Lanie Phelps used to share. But at least Lanie was age-appropriate.

"Are you cold?" Amber started to the tuck the beige hospital blanket closer to me. I swatted her away. My head fogged again.

Better stick to what was important. "Do any of you know where my boots are?"

Casey pointed to the corner of the room. My Ariats were sitting neatly by a gray padded chair that had seen better days. I could see a few blood specks, but they appeared otherwise unscathed. I was sure the leather cleaner would fix them right up. If I ever ran into Jesus again, he would be as relieved as I was.

"This is Ed," Dr. Renfroe piped up. He gestured to the other guy in scrubs. He was chunky, like Bryce, and wore brown clogs and a sour expression. Maybe he was aware of how tacky his footwear looked. "He's going to need to ask you a few questions while I check on some other patients. Be sure to answer all of them carefully, okay?"

"Okay, okay," I mumbled, suddenly uncomfortable with all of the attention I was getting.

"I just don't want to take any gambles with a former employee's daughter," Dr. Renfroe said with a smile.

"Not the gambling kind, eh?" I said, simultaneously attempting to humor him and avert my eyes from all that chest hair.

Renfroe kept smiling, but his eyes grew serious. "Not in the least," he said.

"Well, hopefully we'll get you out of here quick," Ed chimed in. "After the questions, we'll run a few more tests."

His name tag indicated that his full title was Ed Lyons, RN. And according to Registered Nurse Ed "Clogs" Lyons, I had already had some blood work and the results were on their way. Soon he would escort me for X-rays, an EKG, and possibly a CT scan. There had been discussion of an MRI, but the consensus was that they needed to wait for the results of the Xray first. (I assumed this meant that they had figured out that the Samuels family was not insured. When you have no money, due diligence becomes statement due, regardless of your personal stand on our national health care system.)

Dr. Renfroe patted me on the shoulder, handed the clipboard to Ed, then made for the other side of the curtain— taking his anti-gambling stance, lousy jokes, and frightening chest hair with him.

RN Clogs handed me a cup. "We'll need a urine sample, too." He offered a bed pan, and then agreed that I could hobble to the bathroom dragging my IV pole and pee in the cup in the handicapped stall.

"I'll help you," said Amber the EMT. She flashed me a smile and held out two tanned, muscular arms.

"Hell no," I heard myself snap. Seriously: Did she really think I was going to let her come into the bathroom and watch me pee? I was not unthankful that she had helped save us, but she was acting like she knew me. She did *not* know me.

"Be nice," my brother said. He was for some reason staring at the ceiling tiles, so I wasn't exactly sure if he was directing the comment to me.

I squinted at Casey some more as Ed hauled me out of bed. My hands were grimy, my teeth were gritty, and unlike my brother I knew that if I sniffed my armpits right now, my nose would hit stink. So how was it that Casey was standing there all new-and-improved when I was sure he had been dead? Had this Amber chick given him a makeover in the ambulance? Maybe that's what came with EMT duties these days. Spruce up the stoner whenever possible. *Aha.* That's probably why he looked so peaceful. He'd masked the odor somehow, but there was only one thing that made my brother peaceful these days. Weed. Maybe EMT Amber was also a dealer. Maybe *that's* how they knew each other.

"You sure you don't need help?" Nurse Ed asked, clogging his way into my train of thought. He did not seem bothered that I was going into a public restroom in my bare feet. I decided to ignore him. I wanted my boots back.

BY THE TIME I returned bearing my cup of green-tinged urine, my blood work had come back from the lab. Ed informed me that my electrolytes weren't so hot, but my blood sugar and liver enzymes were normal. He slapped an ice pack on my bruised shoulder and commented that he had never seen anything like my pee before and that I might have to see a specialist.

"She already has," Amber told him.

Casey looked startled. Me, too. He caught me staring at him.

"Amber hung out with me in the waiting room," he said.

Before I could question him about this bizarre explanation that explained absolutely nothing, RN Ed began interrogating me about my diet. Having now been up close

and personal with my pee, he seemed convinced that I was consuming algae or seaweed.

"Are you sure you don't eat sushi?" he kept repeating. He shifted from one ugly clog to the other as he scribbled on my chart. "Or maybe oysters? Have you had Gulf oysters lately? Personally, I haven't touched them since Hurricane Ike. God only knows what's in the water. And the ones from around Louisiana and Alabama are just as bad. All those lab animals that went loose after Katrina hit New Orleans? Same thing."

I decided that the clogs were making Ed cranky. Just because the Crocs kiosk in the mall was still in business did not mean that one had to shop there. I chose not to share this observation with Ed. Anyone who thought that Gulf oysters could make your pee look like St. Patrick's Day beer was probably not interested in my fashion tips.

At some point, Casey and Amber excused themselves to go wait for Mom in the ER lobby. My eyes narrowed. I was torn. I didn't see why he needed Amber Velasco, EMT, to help him wait, but if it gave me a break from watching her ogle my brother like 1) he was cute or 2) he was about to discover the cure for cancer or 3) both, I was all for it. If she *was* a weed dealer, I couldn't imagine she'd be pleased with him. He wasn't exactly rolling in money. I knew this for a fact because he always bummed pot from Dave. Long story short: Amber Velasco gave me the willies.

Ed and I carried on without them. He was just finishing his checklist and clogging toward the curtain when Mom shuffled in. Casey held her by the elbow. Tears stained her cheeks. She was still dressed in her baggy sweats and the pink Tee, and had shoved her feet into an old pair of flip-flops. She looked like, well, a homeless woman.

Amber trotted behind them, her EMT pants still perfectly creased.

"Jenna," Mom said in a papery thin voice. She patted my hand. Her fingertips were dry, and the skin around her thumbnail was red and raw like she'd been picking at it. I was glad Dr. Renfroe had left. I didn't want him to see her like this.

"I'm fine," I said. My head gave a throb and for a second I thought I might puke again, but I forced a smile. "Nurse Ed here's taking great care of me."

"Has your daughter consumed Gulf oysters lately?" Ed asked. He frowned at the clipboard, waiting for Mom to enlighten him.

Instead, she started shaking. "I have to go home," she hissed. Her voice quavered. Her glassy eyes bulged, staring at a spot above my pillow, at nothing. Suddenly, she was somewhere else. "I have to go home. You take care of your sister, Casey. I can't be here. I'm sorry."

She whirled and shuffled back through the curtain.

Casey followed.

Thanks, Mom! Love you, too!

I closed my eyes. I hadn't cried in front of Renfroe—who at least I sort of knew—and I was absolutely not going to cry in front of Oyster Ed, who I didn't want to know at all. He wore clogs. He asked stupid questions. He did not merit a cry.

Somehow the papers got signed and permission to do whatever it was they were doing to me, confirmed. Our lack of health insurance was also once again documented. I must have dozed for a few minutes, because suddenly Casey was beside me again.

"Taxi waited for her," Casey said.

I wondered if maybe it was that guy Wayne. He could show Mom his prosthesis and cheer her up.

"He gave us an emergency discount," Casey added. "Real nice of him."

Huh, I thought. Probably not Wayne then.

The curtain rustled and Amber returned. I decided that her dark blue eyes were creepy. Yes. That settled it. She was a drug dealer with creepy eyes. She'd sold my brother marijuana to keep him calm. Or given him a freebie. It was the only explanation.

A LITTLE AFTER one in the morning, Dr. Renfroe reappeared to join Amber, Casey, and me in the too-small hospital room. He expressed his surprise that I did not have a concussion and pulled out my IV.

"Sorry I missed your mother," he said. "Ed tells me she was here."

"Excuse me, Doctor," Amber said, pointing at something on my chart. "Jenna's vitals still aren't what they should be. I think Ed should have ordered some more blood tests."

So now she wanted to poke more holes in me. And so, it seemed, did Dr. Chest Hair Renfroe. He actually agreed with her.

Three vials later, I was finally released.

"He'll call you tomorrow with the results," Amber told us as Casey helped me shove my feet back into my Ariats. "In the meantime, get some rest, okay?" She handed Casey a sack. "Two turkey sandwiches, two bottles of water, and two individual packs of Chili Cheese Fritos," she said and smiled. "You should eat. You both must be starving."

I knew I should probably thank her for the food. It *was* nice. On the other hand, why was she hanging around us, encouraging Dr. Renfroe to do more work on my behalf? True, I was probably still dying from not-Exploding-Head-Syndrome, but I wondered if this was part of the standard EMT gig. It didn't seem likely. I imagined she probably had other people to drag from drifting, crappy Priuses.

Casey said it for me. "Thanks, Amber. We should go."

"Of course," she said.

He nodded. "I'll do better next time."

I frowned. Better at what? Not crashing our car? Paying her back for the weed?

Amber looked mildly amused.

"C'mon," Casey put his arm around me and helped me walk out to the parking lot. The outside world seemed a lot brighter than I expected it to at one-thirty in the morning. My legs were suddenly very tired again, and we stopped a couple of times for me to catch my breath. My brother stroked his hand over my hair. He still smelled very good. That strange look was back on his face.

"Jenna," he said. "I—"

"You're gonna be looking a long time," called a voice from behind us.

What do you know? Amber Velasco, starting to verge on stalker, strode up to us. "Your car isn't here, remember?"

We did remember . . . Now. Casey's face flushed a little in the harsh fluorescent glow. Maybe he was embarrassed that he'd totally zoned out about the wrecked Prius. I honestly had no idea what was going through his head, other than scoring more weed or possibly uploading pictures of this chick, something that I definitely did not want to think about.

"Your house is only a couple of miles out of my way," Amber added gently. "It's no trouble." I was too exhausted

to ask how she knew or how it was that the red Camaro parked a few feet from us was hers. I just let the two of them fold me into the front seat and then closed my eyes for the ride.

MOM WAS ASLEEP when we got home. I'd harbored a distant fantasy that with Casey's freakish transformation, Mom might have morphed back to normal on the return taxi ride. That got squashed the moment I saw her huddled on her bed, the TV still on.

Here was the truth: Dad was gone, no matter what Mom had rambled incoherently at me before today's catastrophe (Correction: yesterday's.) Mom was never going to be herself again. I might as well accept it. But the truth not only sucked, it also confused me all over again. Why the hell *had* Dad disappeared five years ago? He had a family. He had a job. He was a sports reporter for the *Chronicle*. He had even published a book on the history of Texas barbeque which you could still find in some stores: *Texas Q: 60 Different Sauces, But Only One Truth*.

People like that—people with homes and vacation plans for Disney World—do not walk out of the house one morning and never come back. They do not leave a note on the kitchen table that cryptically says, "Y'all take care. I love you," underneath which they place a certificate for a fajita dinner for four at Manny's Real Tex Mex in the city. (Coincidentally, Dad had been working on a new book about Mexican food when he flew the coop.) By the time we realized that his departure was permanent, the gift certificate to Manny's had expired.

But that was the whole point. I could drive myself crazy over the past. Sixty different possibilities, but only one truth.

He was gone. And in the here-and-now, we had no car and virtually no Mom.

Casey and I sat at the kitchen table and ate our turkey sandwiches and chips. (I let him have both packs.) We drank our waters. Neither of us spoke. My brother kept eyeballing me like I was going to explode or something.

"I never saw that pickup truck," he said finally. "I just wanted to get you to the hospital, Jenna. I swear." He chugged the rest of his water. I watched him swallow. He looked upset, worried—and something else I couldn't name.

"I know," I said.

My brother wadded up the sandwich sack and tossed it in the general direction of the kitchen counter. Obviously his guilt about almost squashing me while I was already dying of not-meningitis had not made him any less of a pig. Which in a way, was a relief. Everything felt so weird right now, *too* weird. But he was the same old Casey, even if he'd been fixed up at the hospital so well that Amber, highly annoying EMT, deserved a medal. Maybe that's all it was with Casey and her. He was just grateful. I'd been so sick, I'd just forgotten that he wasn't all *that* out of shape before the accident. I was sick, so I wanted him to be sick, too. I was "projecting," something Mr. Collins had accused me of doing when he assigned my detention. This was fancy talk for saying that the only reason I'd called him an asshat was because my family was screwed up.

I had informed him that I did not need to be psychoanalyzed. He had been impressed by my vocabulary.

"You want me to sleep in your room?" Casey asked, helping me upstairs.

I frowned at him. "Um, no."

He laughed. I noticed that his chipped lower front tooth was no longer chipped.

"Did you file your tooth?" I reached out to touch it and he backed away.

Okay then. Casey retreated to his own room.

I was already half asleep as my head sank into my pillow.

IT WAS STILL dark outside when something woke me. I realized that I had to pee, so I started toward the bathroom when I noticed light shining from under Casey's door. (Let me add here that sharing a bathroom with Casey has not been the highlight of my existence. This includes but is not limited to my distaste for the permanent yellow stain at the base of our mutual toilet because my brother is incapable of aiming into the bowl.) That's when I heard noise coming from Casey's room. Voices. Was he really up at four in the morning listening to Katy Perry again?

I stood in the hallway, listening.

No. Not Katy Perry, just the same floaty, droning drum-filled instrumental stuff that I'd heard after the accident, coming from the ambulance. And the voices: one was Casey's of course. The other sounded like . . . Amber.

Okay. *Now* it made sense. He'd figured out what music she liked, found pictures of her online and was putting on a little show for himself. Amber might be a drug dealer, but I had to admit she was good looking, maybe even the cheer type, like stupid Lanie Phelps. I bet Casey found some of her old high school photos. That had to be it. Yes, it was gross and disturbing. But it was logical.

I pressed my ear to the door. The white glow seeped out onto my bare feet. My toenails sparkled.

"I can't be," I heard Casey say.

"But you are," said the voice that sounded like Amber. "Get used to it."

Wait. Was she actually in there with him? No way. But her voice definitely didn't sound like it was coming though his crap computer speakers. My head spun, and not from not-Ebola. I was too confused. My brother was not what one would define as a chick magnet. He hadn't even *wanted* a girlfriend since Lanie dumped him. (As if he'd had a choice! He was practically my legal guardian, except for the legal part.) Plus let's face it, Casey found it acceptable to wear a shirt with a Hostess Twinkie on it. He did not have middle-of-the-night visits from older women with gainful employment and an EMT uniform. Unless said women came to sell him weed. Right. That had to be it.

My heart pounded. I figured I'd give them fair warning.

"Casey." I rapped sharply on the door. "What's all that racket?"

The noise stopped abruptly, like turning off a faucet. The light went dark. I opened the door to Casey's room.

He was sprawled on his back in his bed. Asleep. Alone. I tiptoed around the room a few times to make sure.

I shook my brother awake. "Was your computer on?" I asked him.

"You must have been dreaming," Casey said. "Do you need me to help you back to your room?"

This wasn't worth answering. I slammed his door behind me, stomped into the bathroom, peed loudly, flushed twice, and stomped back to my room.

The universe had spit out something. And no, it was not my not-Ebola and my runaway father and incapacitated mother. I had no clue *what* it was. At least not yet.

Jenna's Journal

December 6th

I am not usually a list girl. But I needed to organize all the weirdness. Maybe if I put it in categories, it really *would* make sense—like an algebra problem or one of those optical illusions—like the one where if you look at it one way it's a lady sitting at a mirror and if you squint just right, it's a skull.

So: categories. They had to help.

1) Amber's email:

Normally I don't read my brother's email. I have enough disturbing stuff in my world. But when I woke up again and heard Casey in the shower, I figured it wouldn't hurt to poke around his room while he was otherwise occupied—and risk touching a laptop still in dire need of disinfectant. That's when I found this:

Email from Amber Velasco, Nosy, Annoying, Possibly Weed-dealing Paramedic

From: Avelasco@me.mail.com
To: csamuels@me.mail.com
Re: Your sister . . .

Just checking on your sister. I don't usually do this, but . . . I snagged your email from the hospital report. I hope you don't mind. If you need anything or have any questions, feel free to call me. And if you want to talk face-to-face, I tend the bar on Saturday and Sunday nights—sometimes also Wednesdays—at Mario's Grille. Just come on in. I'll be looking for you.

~Amber Velasco, EMT.

I'll be looking for you.

Really, Amber? Subtle. She wasn't asking Casey to meet her. She was telling him. So he *must* have owed her money, or something. At least she had sort of asked about me. Conclusion: Maybe she wasn't an entirely evil weed dealer. People can be all sorts of things. Just look at the Samuels family.

2) My brother's outfit and Dave's Grandma's car:

After I nosed around Casey's laptop, I hiked downstairs to check on my mother. She was wearing the same pair of sweats but had now changed into a Green Lantern T-shirt Casey had outgrown. She seemed only vaguely aware that I had had some kind of seizure in her presence yesterday. Even foggier was the memory that she had called BJ's hysterical

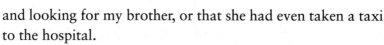

and looking for my brother, or that she had even taken a taxi to the hospital.

I got her to eat some toast and take a vitamin. I figured it would be pointless to show her the hospital bill that would now be added to the mountain-sized pile of things we hadn't paid. Then I trudged back upstairs, just as my brother strutted out of his room.

He was wearing clean jeans and an unwrinkled, collared khaki shirt. Strutted might not be the best description. Hip-swaggered probably covered it more accurately. Where had he gotten this shirt? Who had ironed his jeans? Why was he walking like that? I decided to stick with something he might actually answer.

"How are we getting to school?"

"No worries." Casey waved his hand, shooing my concern like he'd shoo a fly. "I talked to Dave. Mamaw Nell is loaning us her Mercury for awhile."

Mamaw Nell was Dave's grandmother. She was eighty-two, weighed about one hundred and five pounds soaking wet, chain-smoked Pall Malls, and had a voice that sounded like metal dragging across gravel. Dave had lived in the spare bedroom of her patio home since his parents kicked him out of the house last year. Either Mamaw Nell was a saint or she had a greater tolerance for Dave's pharmaceutical activities than the generation between them. I had never quite decided.

Casey looked both uncomfortable and smug. Was such a combo even possible? Maybe it was more like embarrassed at his wonderful new self-confidence. I'd be embarrassed if I were him, maybe just on general principle. He rubbed his neck and fiddled with his collar. A horn blasted on our driveway. Dave and the Mercury had arrived.

Mom had already retreated to her room. The muffled sounds of *The Price is Right* echoed from behind her door.

Outside our house sat a copper-colored car the size of a small boat. The Prius, had it not been at Lonnie's Body Shop on Rayford Road receiving its last rites, would have beeped its uninspired little horn in awe. Also, the Prius would have called Dave an asshat for bashing its sad little self into the Jack in the Box menu in the first place.

We climbed inside. Dave let me ride shotgun. The car smelled like margaritas and mothballs. Mamaw Nell—Dave told us by way of explanation when I gagged and threatened to upchuck on the front seat—made frequent trips with her bunko group to the gambling boat on Lake Charles to play the nickel slots.

"Doesn't your grandma need her car?" I asked, trying to speak and hold my breath at the same time. Dave's ancient Corolla, I knew, was finally out of the shop. Why hadn't he just given us a ride?

"Yeah, well, it was freaky, if you want to know the truth," Dave said with a stoned chuckle. He slumped back in the seat cushion, one hand lazily on the wheel. "I was in the bathroom when my cell phone rang. When I came out, there she was, talking to your brother and offering him her car." He turned to Casey. "What all were you saying to her, anyway? After you hung up she was going on and on about how, like, amazing and polite you are. And I was like, 'Do you know him, Mamaw?' Anyway, here it is. She says y'all can keep it as long you need to."

I figured my brother would question this gift. Casey had his problems, but even he knew that Dave was a pot-smoking loser who frequently manipulated the truth to suit his better interests. He'd even attempted to teach me to roll joints

one night, even though I didn't smoke the stuff, causing my brother to blacken Dave's left eye.

"You know what?" Casey reached over from the back-seat and put his hand on Dave's shoulder. "Why don't you let me drive?"

"Better driver than you," Dave drawled.

But he slammed to a stop when Casey squeezed his shoulder again.

"Damn," Dave said. "What the hell? You been working out or something?"

"Something," my brother said.

Dave let Casey drive the rest of the way to Ima Hogg. Yes, I know this should have made me nervous. But it didn't.

One more thing: Mamaw Nell had sent Casey—not me—a tin of her famous snickerdoodles. And a Starbucks gift card. Yes, my brother had emerged unscathed (improved, even) from a car wreck, but he got the free car and the get-well gifts.

Conclusion: Mamaw Nell, like her grandson, was an asshat.

3) How Maggie reacted:

Mags was standing near the front door of Ima Hogg scribbling on a piece of paper when the three of us pulled up.

"Maggie," I hollered, staggering out of Mamaw's car, trying to escape the mothball/booze aroma wafting after me.

It had been too late to call her when we'd got home. (Besides, in one of her final coherent moments, Mom had refused to let me own a cell phone before I got to high school. I'd been furious about this until we went broke. After that, I saw it as one less thing I had to give up.)

"You're supposed to be in Spanish," I said.

"I am." She gestured to a group of kids over by the flower beds. "Señora Flanagan is having us list the Spanish words for everything we see." Maggie's eyes widened. "What happened to you?" As Maggie stared at me, I stared back. She wore knee-high black Converse, fish nets, a black cotton short skirt, a sparkly navy tank top, and a magenta hoodie that covered not only her out-of-dress-code sleeveless shoulders but also the against-Ima-Hogg-policy henna tattoo she'd recently gotten above her left boob. Maggie was a fashion original.

Maybe that's why we're best friends: we don't look or dress at all alike. Maggie is short but mighty—exactly 5' 2 ½" tall, with chin-length blonde hair, currently dyed brick red with a black streak down one side. I am taller—about 5' 7" with the option of a final growth spurt still open. My features are more forgettable: no tats, no dye, shoulder-length brown hair and brown eyes. I'm on the thin side, but I've got really strong legs. Or at least I used to before I started dying of whatever it is I'm dying of.

I began to update Maggie on the insanity of the accident and its aftermath, until I noticed that she was only sort of listening. Mostly what she was doing was gaping at my brother as he hopped out of the car.

"Hey, Mags." Casey mustered a grin. He cocked his head. "Nice tattoo."

His hair was particularly wavy, which I chalked up to Houston December humidity. But his eyes were still bright and sparkly, like yesterday. Again, I came to the logical conclusion: Amber must have hooked him up with better quality pot. One that was lighter on the side effects. Or maybe it was just a trick of the light, which somehow seemed brighter around my brother. Dave's eyes, on the other hand, were

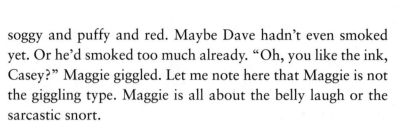

soggy and puffy and red. Maybe Dave hadn't even smoked yet. Or he'd smoked too much already. "Oh, you like the ink, Casey?" Maggie giggled. Let me note here that Maggie is not the giggling type. Maggie is all about the belly laugh or the sarcastic snort.

My eyes followed Mags's eyes to the chest area under my brother's unwrinkled polo. When had he acquired what looked like sort of six-packy abs instead of his normally blobby, too-many-Jack-in-the-Box-tacos middle? Right, I already knew: I just hadn't noticed, given that I was dying and he always wore loose-fitting clothes. Carrying those trays of barbeque at BJ's must be more of a workout than I thought. I squinted at him in the sunlight. This I wasn't imagining: he'd groomed his eyebrows. No. That had to be from the hospital. Maybe Nurse Ed had plucked a few strands while he was scrubbing the blood off Casey's face. You just never knew with those Crocs folks.

I yanked on his sleeve. "Can I talk to you for a second?"

Casey ignored me. "What?" he said genially, still smiling at Mags.

I decided to look up brain injuries at lunch. Most likely the hospital had missed something. There was no other way to explain Casey's freakish change in behavior, or his sudden improvement in the posture and hygiene department.

"Maggie is off limits," I hissed, loud enough for her to hear too. "Leave the felonies to Dave, okay?"

"Hey," Dave said. He'd moved up to the driver's seat. "Highly uncalled for. Besides, you could take a few lessons from her in the outfit department." He eyeballed my boobs, then opened the little tin and popped one of Casey's snickerdoodles into his mouth.

That was Dave. For all I knew, he'd smashed our car into

that Jack in the Box menu because that's what Dave did when someone was nice to him. Dave was screwed up like that. Which made the whole Mercury loan thing even weirder.

That strange look crossed Casey's face again. "Go to class, Jenna. You're already way late. I'll pick you up at five, okay. Just like we planned. If you feel bad, just go to the nurse and tell her to call my cell. I'll come for you. Don't worry."

He reached up and pressed his hand to my cheek.

His palm was warm. I brushed his hand away. My brother was not the touchy-feely type. Neither was I. But even as I thought about calling him on the fact that he was trying something shifty—while, I might add, trying to make me ignore that, yes, he'd been hitting on my best friend—I felt the wiggly knot in my stomach ease.

Dumbfounded, I stared until he and Dave and the Merc disappeared in a cloud of exhaust.

"What's with your brother?" Maggie asked.

I shrugged, unable to answer. The wiggly knot started forming again. It wasn't just that Casey was not himself in more ways than I could name. It was what I felt when he rested his hand on my face. The closest I could come to remembering what it felt like was eating birthday cake, back before Dad ran off. It wasn't just warm on my insides. It was warm *inside* the insides. This weird peaceful feeling that started in my toes and migrated straight to the top of my head.

I was not a peaceful person. Maybe I had been once in the days of Dad. But that was so long ago, I didn't really remember. What I did know is this: Casey's hand on my face also felt like Christmas morning, acing a math test, and having my mother brush my hair until it was shiny (also, needless to say, something I barely recalled) all rolled up in one.

"I wish I knew," I finally told Maggie. And I realized right then and there that I had to get to the bottom of Casey's bizarre change, and I had to do it soon. Something was coming or something was behind it. But like any optical illusion, I just hadn't looked at it the right way.

4) What happened in Algebra:

"You're tardy."

This is what Mr. Collins told me as I tried to sneak in at 9:25, exactly five minutes before the end of class. He did not ask me why. He did not ask me about my swollen eye or my general pale and hanging-on-by-a-thread appearance. He did not even comment that at least my boots looked good, which he should have since I had shined them up and removed the blood spots.

"I *should* mark you absent," he finished.

I resisted the temptation to point out that Corey Chambers was asleep and drooling on his desk. Corey roused himself as I walked toward my seat and gave me a halfhearted wave. Like my brother, Corey scored his weed from Dave. (Or like my brother used to, before he met Amber Velasco.) This seemed to make him feel that we had stoner solidarity. I wished it hadn't.

Mr. Collins wrinkled his forehead, considering what he should do with a juvenile offender like me. Or maybe that constipated expression owed to something not on my radar: he'd had a fight with the wife, or the principal had informed him that Sansabelt slacks were on sale at Penney's and he was trying to figure out how to work in a trip to the mall during his off period.

With teachers you just never know.

Or people in general.

"I do believe," said Mr. Collins, tapping his stubby fingers on his desk as the clock ticked audibly toward the half hour, "that you, Miss Samuels, are going to owe me another afternoon of detention."

I bit my lip, forcing myself not to call him an asshat. Better to pretend that he didn't exist. The next four minutes crawled with excruciating slowness until the bell rang. Everyone scattered like buckshot.

"Asshat," I said under my breath.

"What?" asked Mr. Collins over the commotion.

"I was in a car accident," I said. "We were at the hospital until like two this morning. Our Prius was totaled."

Mr. Collins popped a couple Tic Tacs into his mouth. Straightened a pile of papers on his desk. "Was your brother driving?"

I didn't answer. I sank deeper into my desk chair. Suddenly, we were alone in the classroom.

"Jenna." Mr. Collins sighed. "What's going on at home? Are y'all okay?"

I was absolutely not going to cry in front of the maybe not so much of an asshat.

"We're fine," I lied to him. "Totally fine. Casey's working at BJ's now, you know."

Mr. Collins considered this. His second period class began filing in. I needed to get to English. I needed to talk to Maggie some more. I needed a lot of things, really. I stood and hurried up the aisle past him.

"I like the boots," Mr. Collins remarked. "They're looking really sharp."

"Thanks."

"You still need to do those two days of detention, by the way."

I paused at the door.

"School policy, Jenna. You cannot call your teacher an asshat. We frown on that here at Ima Hogg."

For a second I thought he was going to hug me. Fortunately, he did not.

"Casey okay?" he asked instead.

I nodded. Casey was remarkably okay. My gut was telling me that this was not really possible. But I wasn't sure how to form that into a response. Or if I even should.

"Take care of that swollen eye," Mr. Collins said as I turned to head upstream against the horde of algebra-knowledge seekers. "I'm here if you want to talk," he added.

"Better block out a lot of time," I told him.

He frowned, but did not otherwise pursue.

What Happened Yesterday and Why I Never Made it to My Detention:

After my five quality minutes with Mr. Collins, I proceeded to English and Maggie—who seemed kind of embarrassed that she'd acted so addle-brained and flirty. We discussed my brother in a series of scribbled notes. This, while we were supposed to be doing grammar worksheets. (Worksheets are big at Ima Hogg. So are Projects. Especially Group Projects. Ima Hogg believed in collaborative learning—which never failed to piss me off every time I got stuck doing work for the Collaborative Slackers.) In the spirit of Ima Hogg educational policy, I labeled our notes like this:

**Jenna and Maggie's Collaborative Attempt to
Analyze Casey's Weirdness**
Me: Does Casey seem different to you?
Mags: Different how? Taller?
Me: Yes! And nicer maybe?

Mags: Idk. Cuter? Seriously. What did he do to his hair?

Me: Idk! Gag. Do you really think he's cute?

Mags: Um. Oddly. Yes. Too weird, right? I mean it's Casey.

Me: Yes! Too Weird. Going to pretend I didn't read that. Do you think it's a brain injury? Maybe he hit his head during the accident and now he's acting all strange?

Mags: Maybe. But how does this explain the hair? And did he whiten his teeth or something?

We would have gone on, but our teacher Mrs. Weiss caught us. She also informed us that our knowledge of the parts of speech was more crucial than my "personal crisis." Her words. Thanks for that, Mrs. Weiss. Asshat is a noun, by the way. In case you were wondering.

Then the bell rang.

"I don't know what got into me," Maggie said as we slogged through the crowded halls to science class. "He just looked nicer or something. Not like himself." She blushed a little and tugged her hoodie over the henna tattoo. "No offense to your brother or anything. Plus even if I was older, Casey's not the kind of guy I'd go out with. Unless that's what the universe wants for me. I guess then I'd have to embrace it."

I decided there was a lot of momentary insanity going on. "No worries." I said.

"What did your mom say about the car?"

I frowned. "If you had to take a guess?"

Maggie nodded, her face softening. She knew the deal with mom. But she was hopeful enough to keep asking. She truly believed that at some point the universe would take pity on the Samuels family and cough up an explanation.

"So what are y'all going to do?" she asked. "Borrow Dave's grandma's car forever? You and Casey can't just go on taking care of everything by yourselves. You had a car accident for God's sake."

I shrugged. What could I do? Mom was Mom. Other than that brief moment yesterday, the last time she had acted like an actual parent had been when Casey quit football. She'd stopped going to work about six months earlier, but she hadn't yet removed herself from our lives. Six months ago, she still occasionally cooked a meal or did laundry or asked us about school. So she knew that our bank account was draining faster than our household income, even if she either wouldn't or couldn't explain how there had been such a sizeable amount of money in there in the first place. Dad had been gone a long time.

"Tell your coaches," Mom had begged Casey when he let it slip that he'd given up football and started waiting tables. "Maybe they'll let you work something out."

Casey refused. It wasn't like he was the star of the team, he'd told Mom. What went on in our house was none of their damn business.

But people knew we were in trouble. Like Mr. Collins, asking if we were okay. Or Dr. Renfroe stopping by to say hi every few weeks or so. For a while he encouraged Mom to get a checkup, to see if the doctors could figure out why she was slowly melting away from planet Earth. I think he knew she wouldn't go, though. He extended Mom's health insurance—which also covered Casey and me—as long as he could, but eventually, she stopped going to work altogether. There was nothing he could do.

Maybe I needed to adopt Maggie's universe philosophy after all. It might make things easier when my family continued to act like a pack of lunatics. Although what did that say about me? Did the universe think I needed this? Maybe the universe needed a kick in the ass from my boots.

Mags patted my shoulder as we slunk into the science room. If I had false teeth like Mamaw Nell, they would have fallen out of my mouth. (Mamaw Nell has three fake molars on the left side. She blames this on a lifetime obsession with cane sugar Dr. Pepper, which—this part is totally gross—she prefers to heat on the stove before she drinks.) Standing in front of the room wearing her EMT uniform and talking to Mrs. Drummond—I shit you not—stood Amber Velasco.

She flashed me that pristine cheerleader smile. "Hey Jenna." She waved. Her ponytail gave a little bounce, but those perfectly smooth bangs stayed perfectly smooth. It annoyed me. *She* annoyed me. What was Amber Velasco, EMT and likely weed dealer, doing in my Ima Hogg honors science class?

"Who is that?" Maggie whispered.

"Amber. The paramedic who rescued me from the Prius."

"I'm today's guest speaker," Amber announced, as much to the class as to Mags and me.

We never had guest speakers. Not unless you counted the ex-drug addicts who came for Red Ribbon week and encouraged us to say no to drugs by wearing crazy socks, pinning red ribbons on our clothing, and having a "craziest red hat" contest. Still, following up drug addicts with a drug dealer seemed grossly negligent, even for Ima Hogg.

On her utility belt, Amber's cell began to blink its little red light. She pulled it out of its holder. Cell phones were a no-no at Ima Hogg.

"I'm looking at her," she said to whoever had called. "I'll ask." She turned to Mrs. Drummond. "You don't mind, do you? This will take just a minute."

Mrs. Drummond pursed her lips—which she really shouldn't do because it makes her lipstick slip into the little wrinkles—but didn't protest.

Amber handed me the phone. "Your brother wants to say hello."

My imaginary false teeth threatened to fall out again.

"Hey, Jenna." Casey's voice boomed into my ear. "You feeling okay?"

"Um, yeah?" Was I really standing here in science class with Amber Velasco, talking to my brother on her cell phone about my general well-being?

"You sure?" he pressed.

Well now that he mentioned it, I wasn't feeling that hot. My foot rash was acting up; I was thirsty again, and my pee had resembled lime-aid this morning. (Yes, I was now a person who studied my pee before flushing.) But why was Casey calling? How did he know that Amber and I would be in the same room? Casey did not know my schedule. Casey did not care about my schedule. Casey cared about weed and Internet porn. What the hell did Amber have on him, anyway?

"I'm okay," I said. "What do you want?"

There was silence on Casey's end. I heard him clear his throat. "I love you," he said. "I was worried."

I love you?!? Okay then. He was stoned.

"I have to go. Amber is our guest speaker and I think she needs her phone back." I waited for him to explain why he didn't sound surprised at Amber's appearance. Even stoned, Casey always had explanations. *Especially* stoned.

"I just wanted to check on you," Casey said. Somewhere

in the background, I heard a familiar voice: *"Casey . . . Oh, my, God. Is that you?"*

I frowned. Lanie Phelps. She didn't sound pissed. The last time I'd seen her in person, she'd shouted at my brother that she expected a boyfriend who was "sober and part of a team." Yes, those were two categories that used to include Casey, not that I gave a damn about Lanie's expectations. When I witnessed that dressing-down, I wanted to kick her with the boots I hadn't yet bought from Jesus. Casey hadn't *quit*; he'd sacrificed. For me. For us. Who wouldn't want to get stoned with a family to take care of? Okay, not that I condoned, but I understood. Which Lanie didn't. No, when Casey had given up on sobriety and sports, she had given up on him. I hated her for that.

"Casey?" I asked. "Casey?"

Nothing. Dead air. Had he hung up on me?

I handed the phone to Amber. I walked to my seat. I sat down. I felt as if I were watching myself in a lame TV show, and I was a walk-on character I knew nothing about.

"Is something going on?" Maggie asked worriedly. She slid into the desk next to mine. Bad move: It was not her seat, so there was a brief but heated negotiation with Ryan Sloboda. "Shoo," she told him, flicking her wrist. "Go sit in my seat. It won't bite you in the ass."

Ryan did as he was told. I felt momentarily bad for him. He was a cute guy with a straight-A average and a slight over-bite. Once the braces did their job, he was probably going to graduate to almost hot. Last year, I'd actually sort of liked him. He played defensive line on the B team of the Ima Hogg Razorbacks. (Yes, our school mascot was also a pig. What else would you expect?) If I hadn't figured that I wasn't long for the world, I might have even kept my options open. Ryan

struck me as the kind of guy who wouldn't mind being pursued. He had nicely shaped lips that I maybe once or three times had fantasized about kissing.

"I have no idea," I told Maggie. "But I think Amber is going to tell us about the life of an EMT." *Or she's going to tell us that she has magic powers and is a mind reader with excellent bang-grooming habits,* I added silently. *Maybe she'll let us know what hair products she prefers. You wouldn't want your hair to get in your eyes while you're following me around like a stalker now, would you Amber?*

The bell rang. Mrs. Drummond introduced Amber Velasco. My brother's possible drug dealer then launched into a shockingly professional presentation entitled "What Does an EMT Do?" There was even a PowerPoint. After she was done, we broke up into triads (Mrs. Drummond did not like saying groups of three) and brainstormed all the high school classes that might be helpful if we, too, had an urge to save lives. For the record, our triad (Ryan, who migrated over to us, possibly because he missed his desk, Maggie and me) came up with:

Chemistry
Anatomy
Biology
Physics
PE
Forensic Science
Psychology
Sociology

We also felt that participation in a sport would help with overall fitness. By we, I really mean Maggie and Ryan. The Lanie thing had left me with a sour taste in my dry mouth as far as sports went. I was also too distracted by the fact that of all the classrooms in Texas, or at least in the Houston metroplex, Amber had miraculously ended up in mine. Mrs. Drummond instructed us to give our lists to Amber on the way out. She called this our "exit ticket."

The Ima Hogg faculty was big on trying to make everything sound like a Very Important Activity. They were not fooling anybody with this chicanery. (Chicanery was my favorite word from last week's vocabulary list in English. It meant trickery especially by an official person. *What is up with all your EMT chicanery, Amber?*)

Here is what Amber did not do during her presentation: She did not acknowledge that she had pulled me out of a car last night. She did not tell the class about the accident. She did not explain why she was following me around. Not that I expected her to come through on that last one, but it would have been nice. Weirder still, however, is that Mrs. Drummond did not ask how Amber and I knew each other. She did not question that Amber had let me use her phone or ask who I had been talking to.

"How are you feeling?" Amber asked as I handed in the list that Maggie, Ryan, and I had come up with.

I shrugged, one shoulder only. I appreciated her concern and all, but she didn't belong here and I could not for the life of me figure out what this was really about. She sure as hell hadn't behaved like a stalkerish drug dealer in the last forty-five minutes.

Could she be something else, then? Maybe she'd taken one look at us at the accident and somehow known that we'd basically been taking care of ourselves for over a year. Maybe she was a spy for Child Protective Services. Maybe she was a cop. That made sense. Maybe she was narc. Aha! Yes. That

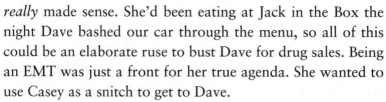

really made sense. She'd been eating at Jack in the Box the night Dave bashed our car through the menu, so all of this could be an elaborate ruse to bust Dave for drug sales. Being an EMT was just a front for her true agenda. She wanted to use Casey as a snitch to get to Dave.

"Is that why you're here?" I hissed at her. "To check on me? To use me to blackmail Casey? I mean, you can't really be an EMT, right? What do y'all do? Take an oath to follow around everyone you save?"

I figured this would piss her off for sure. Or catch her in her web of crazy cop or narc or CPS lies.

But Amber smiled. I thought I saw something flash in her dark blue eyes. "We don't take an oath, exactly." She placed her hand on my arm. She wasn't trying to stop me or hold onto me or anything. It was just a casual gesture. I wanted to shake her off. I couldn't. I was frozen.

A feeling of total calm washed over me. It was a wave of warmth. All the confusion and frustration simmering inside me, all of the worry about Casey, all of it disappeared. The other feelings that I walked around with all the time—sadness and fear and the occasional moment of hopelessness that just possibly the Samuels family was going to end up some sort of statistic other than happy—they vanished, too. Poof. Gone. In their place, came peace. I felt comforted.

Like when Casey touched my face, I thought suddenly. But Casey was my freaking brother. I didn't even know Amber Velasco. What I knew I didn't like or trust. So why did I feel so relaxed? Nothing pisses me off more than not being able to work up the proper emotion. It's part of why a piece of me wanted to smack Mom every time I saw her. Not now, though. Thinking of Mom now, I only wanted to hug her.

"Jenna?" Maggie's voice broke through my happy cloud.

The cement block hall of Ima Hogg's science wing smacked back into view.

Amber slipped her hand from my arm. I had the uncomfortable sensation that I wanted her to put it back. That made about as much sense as everything else. I wanted Amber Velasco to disappear. I wanted things to go back to normal. Minus the not-Ebola.

"You coming to lunch?" Maggie asked. She wagged her finger, a *hey, we've only got twenty-nine minutes to eat* kind of motion.

My head was suddenly foggy and my legs felt heavy in my boots. I think I said goodbye to Amber. Maybe I didn't. She looked like she wanted to tell me something, but I turned and trudged behind Maggie to the cafeteria. The free and reduced lunch line was already snaking out of the food area toward the tables. What I wanted (even though I felt like I was going to puke) was a slice of pizza or maybe a chicken sandwich. What I was going to get was the soft taco plate because that's what the kids in the free and reduced lunch line got on Thursdays.

"See you at the table," Maggie said, heading off to the paradise of food for purchase.

I would have nodded but my vision was going wonky again, and I didn't want to risk more dizziness.

I swayed. Someone grabbed my elbow. Mr. Collins's face swam into view as he hauled me upright. His eyebrows were scrunched tight. Did I look that pathetic? At least he had kept me from being the girl who fell in the Ima Hogg cafeteria.

"You okay, Jenna?"

"No," I said. I was so tired that I couldn't even work up a proper lie.

"You don't look okay," he continued.

"I need to eat my tacos," I squeaked.

"Do you want me to take you to the nurse?" I pulled my arm away. I could feel the Ima Hogg lunch-eating population watching us. My almost passing out might not be as exciting as last week when Jordan Vanderslice beaned Kendall Estes on the head with a burrito, but it was better than nothing. I thought Mr. Collins would argue about the nurse, but instead he tilted his head. His gaze aimed over my shoulder toward the vending machines.

I turned. *Casey?* Amber and my brother were striding in unison across the cafeteria toward me. Their right legs stepped and then their left, like they had rehearsed for a parade or had joined the military. What was Casey even doing here? My vision was bouncing. They looked oddly alike, tan and toned and no hair out of place. How was that possible? Was Amber actually some long-lost Samuels cousin? How was Casey's shirt still so crisp and clean? Wouldn't it have been stained with bong water by now?

Casey landed on my left and Amber on my right. Mr. Collins eyeballed them like they'd arrived from Mars. So did I. They might as well have.

"We need to talk to you, Jenna," Casey said. I really was losing my mind. Casey and this weird chick were a "we" now.

"About what? I have to eat lunch. Why aren't you in school?"

"Did you sign in at the front office?" Mr. Collins stood up taller.

"I need Jenna, Coach," Casey told him. Casey hadn't called Mr. Collins "Coach" since he quit football. "Please," he added.

This was disturbing for two reasons: 1) Casey never said please to anybody. 2) Mr. Collins said, "Okay."

"Thanks," Amber added helpfully. "It's important." She locked her dark blue eyes on Mr. Collins. Then she looked at me. "C'mon," she said.

Like I was going to follow her?

"Maggie's waiting," I said. My insides felt oddly conflicted. Part of me wanted to kick Amber in the shin. The other part wanted to let her hug me. *Narc*, I thought again. *Only explanation: My brother's an idiot. He's been suckered in by her supposed concern. Or he's already been read his rights. Any second now she's going to flash her badge. We'll be arrested. We'll lose our house. We'll—*

"You'll talk to Maggie later. Do you need help walking?" Casey took my hand. Normally, I would not have held my brother's hand in the middle of the school cafeteria. Normally, he would not have offered it. In fact, normally, he might have been the one in need of propping up. But out we walked, hand in hand, Amber trailing behind.

"Your blood test results came back," Casey stated without any small talk. "Dr. Renfroe called me. Jenna. We're taking you back to the hospital."

"Um, what? Why?" I tried to process what was going on.

"We need to get a move on," Amber said, more to Casey than to me.

I dug the heels of my boots into the scuffed tile floor. "What the hell are you talking about? I can't go. I have detention later."

"Detention can wait," Casey said. He extricated his hand and laid that warm, peaceful palm on my shoulder—as still as a glassy pond. "Jenna, someone's been poisoning you."

H ere is What Happened After I Found Out I'd Been Poisoned:

1) I did not go batshit crazy in front of the student body and faculty of Ima Hogg, although I did make a few panicked vowel sounds and I think a couple of nervous consonants snuck out while I was at it. It sounded like: "Uhoheepm."

2) Dr. Renfroe earned his paycheck. (Not that we could pay him, of course. But I pictured buckets of metaphor money falling over his head.)

BEFORE ALL THAT, Maggie caught us trying to escape the cafeteria. She dashed to follow Casey, Amber, and me.

"I'm taking Jenna to the hospital," Casey told her. "She'll call you later." He placed that same hand on Maggie's. She looked sort of startled—like she'd seen a ghost—but then just said, "Okay."

She must have felt it, too. Because somewhere my brain registered that this was not at all like Mags. Unless she thought he was trying to hit on her.

"Do you think it's from the cafeteria food?" I managed as Casey and Amber half-walked, half-dragged me out of Ima Hogg. I was feeling worse. (Maybe because I was being poisoned? Or because I thought I should feel worse now that I *knew* I was being poisoned?)

Amber showed the security guard a piece of paper and he waved us on. This also registered in my head as strange, but I was hyperventilating so it was all I could do to keep walking. Of course it was the Ima Hogg cafeteria food. Mrs. Holtkamp had been a little shifty-eyed lately when she watched me punch in my free lunch number. Damn soft taco plate lunches.

"Don't know," Casey said. He was gripping my left arm, Amber, my right, as they hauled me toward the visitor lot. "Dr. Renfroe needs to do more tests. There's some kind of toxin in your system, Jenna."

"How did it get there? Do you have it, too?"

"No."

"What do you mean, no? How do you know? Did he test your blood?" A worse thought occurred to me. "What about Mom? Maybe that's what's going on with her."

"I'm not being poisoned, Jenna," Casey stated. "I'm positive. I don't know about Mom. We thought of that, too. We'll check it out."

"We *who*?" I may have been losing consciousness, but no blackout was going to keep me from calling him on this "we" BS. "Who *are* you?" I demanded, glaring at Amber.

Casey clammed up. He unlocked the Merc.

"We'll get to that, Jenna," Amber muttered. Her Camaro was parked two cars down. "I'll follow you."

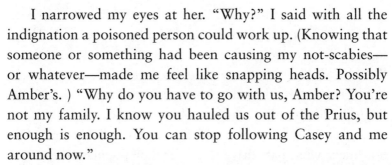

I narrowed my eyes at her. "Why?" I said with all the indignation a poisoned person could work up. (Knowing that someone or something had been causing my not-scabies— or whatever—made me feel like snapping heads. Possibly Amber's.) "Why do you have to go with us, Amber? You're not my family. I know you hauled us out of the Prius, but enough is enough. You can stop following Casey and me around now."

Amber did not respond. She had that same odd look on her face that my brother kept getting. The one that said she knew something that I didn't. Well of course she did. *We'll get to that,* she'd said.

"Just get in the car, Jenna." Casey muscled me toward the rear of the Merc. "We'll sort it out later."

There was nothing to sort out. But I had used the last of my fading energy haranguing Amber. I needed to sit down and catch my breath. Casey opened the door and shoved me inside. "Lie down if you need to."

"I'm fine," I said. I collapsed on the cluttered backseat. My nose wrinkled. My irritated gaze roved over the crap. An empty pack of Pall Malls. A Kit Kat wrapper. A margarita glass. A bunch of pictures of Mamaw and her bunko group, most of which looked like they were taken at a casino. A folded plaid blanket. And on the floor, a balled up Jack in the Box sack that smelled freshly of tacos, possibly the breakfast variety. Dave and Casey must have made a stop after they dropped me off this morning.

I curled up on the seat, pulled the blanket over me (simul-taneously discovering the source of the mothball odor) and flipped through the pictures, trying to ignore the burning sen-sation on the bottoms of my feet. Mamaw sure loved the slot machines. She was posed in front of at least a dozen of them.

I had never gambled. If Dr. Renfroe didn't come up with a cure, I might not get a chance. Not that I cared. I always figured if someone gave me a last wish, I'd ask for Disney World. I did not want my obituary to read: Jenna Samuels, the girl who breathed her last at Isle of Capri Casino. We might be broke, but I was not a low-rent girl.

Casey drove like a proverbial bat out of hell. (Actually, I do not know what bats drive like or if they populate the underworld. I just know that we went fast enough to plant my head in the seat.) I tried not to think about what had happened last night. At least this time, if we hit something or skidded off the road, we had a fighting chance. The Mercury was a beast.

DR. CHEST HAIR Renfroe was pacing the lobby when Casey guided me into the ER. (Fortunately, said hair was concealed under a shirt and tie.) Casey actually tried to pick me up and carry me, but I put up a stink and he let me shuffle in on my own. Amber caught up with us in the same curtained cubicle where I'd been dropped the previous night.

"Have you been to West Texas lately?" Dr. Renfroe asked. "Or to the desert? Arizona maybe? Or New Mexico?"

It was Ed Lyons, RN, interrogation *déjà vu*. Only with a Southwest flavor.

"No," Amber answered for me.

"I can speak," I snapped. She was standing just far enough away that I couldn't kick her. Or pull her still perfectly smooth bangs.

Casey cleared his throat. One well-groomed brow arched. "Why do you ask?"

"Because Jenna's blood test shows traces of snake venom," Renfroe said. "There's something else, too— something we haven't been able to identify. That's why I'm

going to take some more blood. I think I can treat you, but I need to be sure. And we need to understand how this is getting in your system. Tell me again how long you've been having these symptoms."

"Um . . ."

"For about a month now," Amber piped up. This time, even Casey looked annoyed.

"You sure it wasn't three weeks?" I spat. "I thought you'd have an exact day count."

Amber chose not to respond, just looked at me sort of blandly then shifted her gaze to the doctor.

"You should be thanking her," Dr. Chest Hair observed. "If she hadn't convinced me to do these other blood tests, I wouldn't have found it. You didn't present like someone being poisoned. And I was worried about internal bleeding from the accident. Whatever it is, and however it's been entering your system, it's diluted somehow. Snake venom is mostly water anyway. It's the enzymes that cause the destruction. Whatever's gotten into you, it's slow-acting. But I'm fairly certain it's been what's making you sick."

Snake venom? I was being poisoned by snake venom? Somehow I doubted that the lunch ladies at Ima Hogg were skillful enough at chemistry to have caused this. Besides, it was not like my taco plate lunch sat separately from everybody else's. So if it wasn't the food, then what was it?

Dr. Renfroe swabbed my arm and drew some more blood. I turned my head the other way. Amber was actually right; it had been a little over a month. The first day I remember feeling really bad had been the Saturday when Maggie and I had gone shopping for her Halloween costume. Maggie always made a big deal out of Halloween. She liked to dress up as these obscure people that no one had heard of. This year she'd gone as Enrico Fermi, the nuclear physicist who helped create the atomic bomb. Her mother had driven us to the big Salvation Army thrift store in Houston so Maggie could look at their vintage suits and ties. (Maggie was fussy about what she defined as vintage. "Just cause it's used doesn't make it vintage. It has to be authentic." We spent a lot of time looking at frayed labels.)

I'd spent the night at Maggie's. About two in the morning, I woke up totally nauseated. I figured it was the extra-large cheese pizza. Or maybe the nachos that I'd brought from our huge stash of take-out leftovers that Casey kept supplying. Probably wasn't a good idea to add jalapeños and brisket, either. Or top it off with barbequed turkey and fried tofu in black bean sauce and then cover it with shredded cheese. Of course, it turned out that nausea was only the beginning. What I'd thought was just an upset stomach didn't go away. Instead, it multiplied into all my other symptoms, culminating with lime green pee.

But snake venom? If someone was feeding me diluted snake venom (with who knows what mixed in?) then why was I the only one getting sick? There was nothing I ate that wasn't also eaten by other people.

Like Ed the RN, Dr. Renfroe ran through some questions about my eating habits. Was I hungry? How often did I puke? Could I connect the puking to any specific food? Did my tongue swell after eating peanuts? Could I think of a food source that only I consumed? I told him my answers: *Sometimes. Lots. Not really. No. No.* He looked peeved. I guess he was waiting for me to shout something like: *Oh! It was the moo shu chicken. I'm the only one in the northern Houston suburbs who ever orders Beijing Bistro moo shu. Ho Nguyen has some serious explaining to do.*

"My feet hurt," I said. They did hurt. Always. I didn't even bother looking down there anymore. I shoved my feet in my boots and went on with things.

Doctor Renfroe capped the blood vial. He made me press a cotton ball to my arm and then covered it with a Band-Aid. "Your feet?" He set down the tube of blood and looked at me.

I nodded.

"She has a rash on her feet," Casey and Amber said in unison. They looked at each other kind of sideways. The narc scenario seemed likelier and likelier. She must have been tapping his phone. This was bad.

"Let me see," said Dr. Chest Hair. "You didn't say anything about that last night."

"I was unconscious," I grumbled. "I think that got in the way."

He helped me pull off my Ariats. I really loved those boots. Maybe I would shine them up later tonight if we got this whole poison thing under control. I kicked off my socks, too. Then he bent down and lifted my legs and looked at the bottoms of my feet.

"Hmm," said Dr. Renfroe. "Huh."

I hunched over so I could look. Casey and Amber moved in closer. Their shoulders touched as they bent over my feet. Both of them smelled nice, I realized. (This was a relative first for Casey.) Like mountain air maybe. Or one of those Christmas candles in the jars—the expensive ones, not the cheap crap from the Dollar Store. But I still felt like I could barf at any second.

"Ow!" I said when the doctor poked a gloved finger into the sole of my foot.

"Does that hurt?" He poked again.

"You think?" *Yes, it hurt, Doctor Chest Hair. I do not yell "ow" just to hear myself holler.*

"Hmm," he said again. Stuart Renfroe, MD, looked at me. Then he looked over at my Ariats. He looked back at me. He held out his hand. "Give me those boots," he directed Amber. She gave them to him. He peered inside. He flashed his head lamp in there and looked some more. Then he picked up my foot and studied the bottom again. Then back to the boot.

Was there some boot chicanery going on?

Amber grabbed up some swabs from the metal tray on the counter.

"Can you hand me a—Oh. Thanks." Dr. Renfroe took the swabs from Amber. Maybe mind-reading was part of EMT/narc training now. He dipped the swabs inside my boot. Amber took the swabs and sealed them in a baggy. "Do you wear these boots a lot?" he asked me.

"I love my boots."

"You have tiny cuts on your feet, Jenna. Little pin pricks. I think they're from your boots."

"So?"

Dr. Renfroe looked at me like I was particularly dense. "If those swabs show what I think they will, we've found the source of your poison." He frowned at my boots again in case I had still not caught on, which finally I had.

"These?" I nearly shouted. "My boots are poisoning me with diluted snake venom? How is that possible? I couldn't even afford real snakeskin! These are just plain old leather."

My brain began spinning like an out of control Tilt-a-Whirl. Did silver-belt buckle Jesus at Bubba's Boot Town want me dead? This seemed not only impossible but highly ironic. But who else? Nobody else had access to them. My

Ariats were almost always on my feet, unless I was asleep. Dr. Renfroe aimed his little ear-examining pen-light down into the black hole of the left boot.

"Aha," he said.

After that, I got a little too foggy to follow. Apparently there were little stiff threads poking up from the soles that seemed to match the pin pricks. Somehow the insides had been coated with poison, and this was how it was entering my system. At least that was the current theory.

The last thing I remember: My boots were bagged up, too. Ed the RN was called to bring a biohazard sack.

Goodbye, Ariats. I loved you with all my heart before you tried to kill me.

AFTER THAT, I must have napped. When I woke up, a very nice detective whose name totally escaped me asked a few questions and then headed to Boot Town to question Jesus Olivier about my Ariats. Something told me this would be a dead end. Jesus had been so insistent that I come back and buy another pair when I got more money. This did not strike me as the behavior of a man who wanted to poison me. Besides, I had let him step me up to the extra bottle of leather cleaner, hadn't I? There was no reason for him to hold a grudge.

When the cop left, I realized that I had no footwear. Ed the RN came to my rescue.

"Here," he said cheerfully. "I found you a pair of clogs that look like they'll fit."

This was how I left the hospital—wearing somebody else's purple Crocs. I wasn't sure what was worse—knowing I'd been poisoned or having to go out in public in the clogs. It was a toss-up. First, however, I received an IV of antivenin, (it was a crap shoot as to which type of snake), a shot of Cipro (plus two weeks of pills), and a tetanus shot. Dr. Renfroe was keeping the option of a blood transfusion on the table, and he would call us about the new blood test. But if he was right, I should start feeling better. My pee might even stop looking green. Maybe. He wasn't sure of that part. He thought the color could be caused by something else, although he had ruled out Ed's theory of algae or oysters. At that point Dr. Renfroe also proved that he should not leave medicine for a comedy career by referring to my green urine as a "red herring" and then chuckling.

Also, I was warned not to take tranquilizers or antihistamines because they might screw with the effects of the anti-venin.

In short, I would live. At least until whoever had been trying to kill me figured out another way to do it.

Stuart Renfroe, MD, did not say that last part. But in my head I knew it was true. I might be sick and dizzy but I was still a straight-A student.

The wiggly knot in my stomach had returned, possibly a permanent resident. I almost wished Casey would lay his hand on me again.

I clogged my way back to the Merc. *Do your thing, antivenin. I am done like dinner with my not-Ebola.* I pictured the antivenin in purple Crocs like the ones on my feet, only smaller, clogging its way through my system, making me feel better.

Suddenly, I remembered that I had not eaten lunch.

"We need to check on Mom," Casey said. "Amber's gonna take her blood so we can get it looked at. I'd bring her to hospital, but after how hysterical she got last night, I don't think she'd go. This way she won't be scared."

"You're seriously going to let *her* stick a needle in Mom's arm?" I decided it was best if I talked about Amber like she wasn't still standing there with us.

"Jenna," Casey said. His cell phone buzzed. He answered.

"Shit," he said when he clicked off. "It was Bryce. I have to work tonight. Kemp Lundquist has the flu." He seemed to consider something. "You're coming with me. You can do your homework at one of the tables."

"And after that, you'll come by Mario's Grille," Amber added. Her tone was pleasant but firm. Like she was the boss of both of us, or an aunt or something, when she was none of the above. "I'm bartending until midnight."

Casey nodded. I gawked at him. Why the hell was he agreeing with this?

"What for? No!" It is hard to be stubborn in borrowed purple clogs. It is hard to be anything but tired and humiliated.

"How long have your mother and Dr. Renfroe known each other?" Amber asked, ignoring my protest.

"I—what? Why do you care?"

"Just work friends? Or does she see him outside Oak View Convalescent?"

"She sees him when he drops by to visit," Casey said.

I glared at him.

"And when he comes over to your house, how long does he stay?" she asked.

"Hello? Why do you care?" I stomped my foot. She didn't even blink. I made a mental note: Crocs are not intimidating to anyone.

Casey yanked me away, but even he seemed flummoxed. (Incidentally, flummoxed was my second favorite word from last week's vocabulary list. It means very confused. *Your interest in my mother has me flummoxed, Amber Velasco.*)

Amber pursed her lips at the both of us. "Just trying to get all the details."

Question: Why would an EMT-slash-bartender need details? Answer: she wouldn't unless she was a narc. Maybe Dr. Renfroe had noticed something and was on to her. He was a smart guy. He would not fall for her fake EMT chicanery. Or maybe her weirdness was some kind of attempt at trying to move up in the medical world. Maybe she just wanted all the glory for figuring out what was wrong with me and figured if she wormed her way into our good graces by helping Mom, then she could hang around some more until she found a way to take credit for my hopefully miraculous recovery. That's the way some people were. They might look like they were helping you but actually they were in it for themselves.

"See you at your house, okay?" Amber said.

"Okay," Casey said. He hurried me towards the Merc.

Amber waved. Her ponytail bounced in the breeze. The space around her seemed . . . brighter than the rest of the parking lot, even though she wasn't standing under one of those horrible fluorescent lights. I was going to have to get my eyes checked. Maybe Dr. Renfroe knew a good ophthalmologist.

"I don't like her," I hissed at Casey as I hoisted myself into the front passenger seat. "I don't see why you keep letting her hang around. We know what's wrong with me. We don't need her."

He turned the key in the ignition. The Merc coughed into life.

"You don't know everything, Jenna," my brother said mysteriously. "She's cool. Really you're just gonna have to believe me, okay?"

I folded my arms across my chest. No, Casey. It was not

okay. Nothing was okay. I wanted to say all of these things, but I didn't.

"Who would want me poisoned?" I asked. I decided to shift topics. Discussing Amber Velasco, who she really was, and what her possible motives could be for casting some weird mind control spell over my brother would only make me queasy again.

"I'm trying to figure that out," he said.

Something in his voice told me that he really was. Somehow, in one day, my brother had morphed from stoned laptop perv to responsible brother who tried to solve mysteries. It was like we'd fallen into a Scooby Doo cartoon, only without Scooby.

Amber met us outside our house. She shimmied from the Camaro carrying her EMT bag.

I clogged inside, once again trying to pretend she wasn't there. It was the only solution to the problem of her constant presence. Like wearing a stranger's purple Crocs. Sometimes that's just what you have to do.

Mom was in bed. No big surprise. Do we burst out and tell her I'd been poisoned? I didn't want to spook her. She blinked at us as we walked in the room. She was still wearing Casey's old Green Lantern T-shirt. A sticky-looking stain about two inches in diameter—juice? drool? —now graced the middle. For some reason, her computer was up and running and logged onto the Internet. Our neighbors all had wireless; we had discovered it wasn't that hard to mooch onto their connections when we got behind on paying for ours.

Mom's eyes focused on Amber. "Hi?" she said, her voice rising like it was a question.

"This is Amber," Casey said. "She helped us last night when we had the accident, remember?"

"Accident?" Mom tilted her head. "I went somewhere, didn't I?"

Casey reminded her of what had happened. He gave her the short version. Car wreck, hospital, consent form—*remember*? Mom's eyes spilled over with tears. I winced at the dust on the furniture, at my mother lying half propped up in her bed, at the sheets that need washing and the various bottles of over-the-counter medicines and vitamins on her nightstand. Of the things that I didn't want Amber to turn out to be, one of them was a witness to our family's pitiful situation. Too late for that, though.

"Don't worry," Amber said quietly. She stood closer than I wanted, so I edged away, the damn purple clogs heavy on my feet against the carpet that needed vacuuming. "She's going to get better, Jenna. I . . . I just have a feeling."

I socked her in the arm. Hard.

"Jesus!" Casey yelped. "Jenna. What the hell?" His face flushed red. He looked from me to Amber to my mother and then back to Amber.

"Your sister's upset," Amber said. "Let her be."

Now she was defending me? I almost laughed. Mom sat up straighter. Her eyes brightened. I lowered myself to sit on the side of the bed. She took my hands in hers. Her skin was rough, like sandpaper.

"Your father's alive," Mom said. "He really is."

I felt my eyes widen. "You know this?" My mouth went dry.

She nodded. "I do. I told you yesterday, Jenna. I've been searching online." Mom drifted, her gaze wandering from my face to the bed to the ceiling. "I . . . it's just so hard to remember." Tears drizzled down her cheeks. "I think he left me some messages. I think it has to do with Mexico? He's

afraid of something. That's why he hasn't come back. I just don't . . ." She faded again. Her mouth moved, but she didn't form any actual words.

"Mexico?" I shook my head. "Are you saying that Daddy's in Mexico?"

More tears. "I don't know," she wept. "I keep trying to remember, and sometimes I start to, and then it goes. I just can't . . ." She bent at the waist, buried her face in her lap.

"Do you want to go to the doctor, Mom?" For a moment I almost forgot about Amber. Gently, I propped her back up. I knew she would say no. She had been saying no for over a year now. At least she didn't seem poisoned. Basically comatose, yes. In need of a hand to the bed sometimes. Forgetful about flushing. But when I flushed her toilet, her pee looked like regular pee. Her feet weren't rashy, and if she was always thirsty, she was hiding it pretty well. I had to beg her to drink. Just getting her to swallow that daily vitamin was a struggle, but she needed something to keep her going. Dr. Renfroe had suggested many times she suffered from depression. She refused to believe it.

Casey turned to Amber. "What if this isn't just depression?" he asked her. "What if it's something else?"

The hair on my arms stood up. He had said what I was trying not to think. But that's why we'd rushed home in the first place. Because I was being poisoned (keep working, anti-venin) and we were worried that maybe the same thing was happening to Mom. But inside my head, a voice whispered, *"Hey Jenna Samuels, remember Maggie's philosophy of life. There are no coincidences."*

Mom slumped back on her pillows and closed her eyes. I scooted closer to her, and when Amber stepped toward the bed, closer still.

"Let Amber help, Jenna," Casey said. "Please."

It was the "please" that made me ease off the bed. He edged around me and stroked Mom's hair, then pressed his hand to her cheek. She sighed and smiled. Her eyes stayed closed.

My heart gave a smack against my ribs. *I* was the one who always got Mom settled down. Not Casey. He—well—he agitated her sometimes. Like part of her deep down, through the terrible fog, knew that he was doing things that didn't make her happy. The cannabis. The hanging out with Dave. Even if she didn't snap out of it and say something to him, I could always see that he made her edgy. I knew this because her reaction always pissed me off. Casey did everything for her, and she had no clue.

My heart gave another knock when I realized that I hadn't even noticed Amber take Mom's blood. The little tube was in her hand. She popped it into a plastic Ziploc and placed it into her EMT bag. I almost protested but decided against it. Instead I straightened Mom's comforter. Casey set a fresh glass of water on her nightstand. He even used a coaster.

"I've got a friend in the lab," Amber said.

Of course she did. I was too exhausted to put up any kind of fight anymore. I hoped my antivenin was doing its job. Extra fun: I had five pages of algebra problems to do for Mr. Maybe Not Quite an Asshat Collins—plus whatever homework I needed to find out about for the classes I'd missed.

And as for Dad, well, screw him. He had no business showing up in the middle of all this craziness, even as a ghost in some wishful fever dream of Mom's. I had long ago decided that he didn't want to be found. Nothing had ever given me the impression that he was dead. But nothing had ever given me the impression that he wasn't, either. Now I wondered.

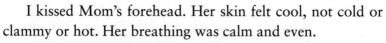

I kissed Mom's forehead. Her skin felt cool, not cold or clammy or hot. Her breathing was calm and even.

We locked up the house and left.

We were two blocks away when I realized that I was still wearing the clogs.

Jenna's Journal

December 7th
LATER THAT NIGHT

What Happened at BJ's BBQ and After (and I swear this is all true):

"Order whatever you want," my brother told me as he directed me to a tiny table for two. "You're hungry, right? You need to eat with that Cipro. I'll bring you a water. You can have a Coke later if you want. But no ice cream if you have cobbler. You can't take that stuff with dairy products."

I smirked. "You a doctor now?"

"Amber reviewed your meds with me." I noticed that the two zits that had sat in the middle of his chin for, well, *ever*, were gone. "Is there something on my face?" Casey asked when I stared for a couple beats too long.

"No."

"Then stop staring. I need to work."

"Who is she?" I demanded. "Seriously, Casey. Enough." I wanted a sandwich, but mostly I wanted the truth, especially if he was now taking medical advice from this stranger who'd inserted herself in our lives. "What's going on with you two? Aren't you pissed that she was nosing around about Mom and Dr. Renfroe? That's not her business. She's like a stalker or something. Doesn't that bother you? Are you in some kind of trouble?"

His face got that weird look again.

Suddenly, I found myself spilling my suspicions. Maybe because for the first time in a month I actually felt decent enough to form coherent thoughts for longer than five minutes, until I had to puke or pee green again. "She's got to be a narc," I said. "Do you owe Dave money, maybe? Is that what she has on you?"

Casey snorted a laugh. "Amber's not a cop. Believe me."

How could he sound so sure?

"Then what? You know something, Casey. So why aren't you telling me?"

"You're just hungry," my brother said calmly. "You've been sick so long you probably forgot how cranky you get when you don't eat. Chopped beef sound okay to you? And fries, right? Jorge's cooking tonight. But remember—"

"Yeah, yeah. No dairy. Got it."

It was official. Casey's overall niceness was weirding me out even more than Amber's stalking. If he was feeling so damn nice, I could use that to my advantage. I would eat and do my homework and eventually wrangle the truth out of him if it killed me. Well, maybe not that.

I MANAGED HALF of the chopped beef without any reversals—impressive since my stomach was still grumbly—and was attempting Jorge's perfectly crisp French fries when I noticed Casey talking to Lanie Phelps over by the drink station. Yes, *that* Lanie Phelps. Blonde-haired, tall cheerleader Lanie Phelps who until yesterday wouldn't have

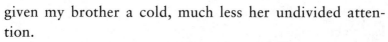

given my brother a cold, much less her undivided attention.

She looked—What exactly? Sad? Embarrassed? She was shaking her head, over and over. Casey was nodding. Then he laid that soothing hand on her shoulder. She stared up at him, eyes wide.

If I hadn't known Lanie better, I might have guessed she was apologizing. But that would be impossible. This was the girl who seemed to prize, above all else, the ability to perform and look good while doing so on *America's Next Sensation* or whatever celebrity-judged talent show was most popular. She was incapable of apologizing. At least she had been back when she'd informed my brother that she did not date loser potheads. I almost wished Amber Velasco could lend me one of her little secret narc hidden microphones (seriously, what *was* in that utility belt?) so I could overhear the conversation.

Then came the truly flummoxing part: Casey leaned over and whispered in Lanie's ear. And she giggled.

I must have gasped, because Casey turned to me.

He pursed his lips. Then he whispered something else in Lanie's ear. She giggled again, this time covering her mouth. Her hand dropped and she flashed another apologetic smile. Casey jerked his head towards the bathrooms and proceeded in that general direction. Lanie followed.

My French fry dropped onto my half-completed algebra worksheet.

I counted. *One Mississippi. Two Mississippi. Three Mississippi . . .*

At twenty, I decided they weren't coming back.

At forty Mississippi I was positive.

All doubt had been removed. The universe had turned against me. What I would give for a freaking cell phone. I needed Mags. *She* could explain these mysteries to me. This *had* to be a sign.

Bryce plodded by. His short-sleeved white shirt gapped a little where it was buttoned over the biggest part of his belly. There were sweat stains in his armpits. I was glad I'd put down the fries.

"Hey Jenna," he said. "How ya feeling?"

"With my fingers," I told him.

He laughed. Bryce found extraordinarily stupid comments highly amusing. It was one of the few things I liked about him. "Where's Casey?" he asked.

Yes, Bryce ran a tight ship here at BJ's. I figured maybe he knew something I didn't. Maybe Lanie was applying for a job. Maybe my brother was showing her how to scrub the toilets. It was possible. Anything was possible. Perhaps this is what the universe was trying to tell me.

Bryce scanned the dining room. "Hmmm," he said. He shambled toward the kitchen. A few seconds later, he headed toward the bathrooms, disappearing down the narrow hallway. I retrieved my French fry, popped it into my mouth, chewed and waited. Another possibility: this was a new and extraordinarily clever method for my brother to ignore my questions about Amber.

All of a sudden Bryce's shouting rang out through BJs: *"Do you still want to work here?"*

An instant later, Casey and Lanie reappeared. Her face was bright red and she was fiddling with her shirt like it needed readjusting, but Casey's hair was un-mussed. So if he wasn't showing her how to scrub toilets, they must not have done too much. But his 'Hi My Name is Dick' nametag sat askew on his chest. Lanie made a beeline for the door and vanished into the night.

"Bye," Casey called after her.

My eyes narrowed. My fists clenched at my sides. There was sparkly peach lip gloss smeared on his left cheek. His grin was wide and happy. Not stoned happy. More like the real thing. So, unless I'd completely lost my mind (wasn't ruling that out) the Ex that "broke my heart forever" (Casey's uninspired phrasing during a cheesy stoned rant) had planted a sloppy smooch on his face. In the BJ's bathroom.

Okay. Deep breaths. Calm down. *Think.* This could explain things: the way he suddenly seemed to care about his appearance, his sudden good mood. Maybe Lanie had called him after he'd nearly died in our car wreck. Maybe she had finally realized what a jerk she'd been. Casey could have kept all this from me, after all. Why not? Maybe he was embarrassed because he knew how much I hated her.

In a way, though, this could be perfect. If he and Lanie were getting back together, it would focus Casey on something besides Amber.

On the other hand—*Really?* Lanie and Casey, reconciled? Last I heard, she'd dumped the star running back at Spring Creek because he was "too short, in the ambition department." Casey had shared this little rumor with me, also when stoned. (Then again, "stoned" could account for most of the last year.) I glanced at the remains of my chopped beef and fries. By now, almost every table was filled with people and platters of sliced beef and ribs and potato salad. There was a line at the door. The tables around me were all Casey's. I saw my chance and leaped from my seat. *Finally.*

While Casey was taking orders, I could corner him. I'd gnaw on his ankles if I had to, but I was not letting him back to the kitchen without telling me something true about Amber and whatever he knew that I didn't. If he ran, I'd chase him.

Besides, no way would Bryce let him leave in the middle of another shift.

Now here is the weird part, which in itself sounds weird. But this was even weirder than poisoned boots and missing fathers, stalker EMTs and gambling grandmas who suddenly loan you their cars, and heinous ex-girlfriends who reappear to possibly hook up with my brother in the bathroom. This was, well—I didn't know *what* it was—which I guess was the point.

I advanced on Casey. We made eye contact. He got that (by now) familiar but strange calm look on his face. Flipped open his order pad. Whipped a pencil from behind his ear. Turned his attention to the family of six crowded around a four top. Launched into his spiel about how BJ's uses mesquite chips in their pit . . .

And that's when it happened.

I was passing by three guys sharing two pitchers of beer and eating ribs. They'd been through a prodigious number of slabs already; bones were piled high on the platter; some littered the table like a barbeque graveyard. One pitcher was empty. The other was full. The chubbiest guy—with a receding hairline that did not bode well for his follicle future—reached for the full pitcher of beer. And I swear on all that is holy that his hand never got to it. I swear that it tipped all on its own. Slid to the end of the table and poured to the floor in a mighty splash as I was speed-walking by.

I slipped. Maybe in the time before persons unknown had tried to do away with me by putting snake venom in my footwear, I might have been agile enough to hop around it. I'd been on the track team after all. I used to be a limber girl. Even Lanie knew that because way back when, she'd been

harping on me to try out for cheer. I was thin and wiry, she'd said. Just right for the top of the pyramid.

But I hadn't been that Jenna in a while. My arms wind-milled. My feet scrabbled in the puddle of beer. I was going down—

And then my brother was at my side.

He caught me by the waist the second before I crashed to the floor. I had been positive that he wasn't even looking my way. Just as positive as I'd been that the pitcher of beer had tipped on its own. Maybe the antivenin wasn't working as fast as I'd assumed, after all.

"You need to be careful," Casey said.

In a daze, I sloshed through the beer back to my table. Casey held my chair, waiting until I flopped into it. "Done with that?" he asked. He removed my dinner basket and scooted off to finish taking the order he'd begun.

AT THE END of Casey's shift, we hauled ourselves into the Merc and drove to Mario's Grille. By then I had recovered my wits enough to work up a new head of steam.

"I know you're holding back on me," I insisted. "You always tell me stuff, Casey. Does Amber have a secret or something? Did she make you take a blood oath or threaten you?" Narcs went corrupt all the time. Especially narcs who were actually dealers. Or worked two jobs, like as an EMT. Or just weird chicks. Yes, I was making it up as I went along, but it sounded way more reasonable than what I'd actually experienced at BJ's.

He laughed, but his jaw flickered. "You're being ridicu-lous, Jenna."

"I'm being ridiculous? This from the guy who lets a stranger take blood from our mother. Amber pops up everywhere! That's not normal." I was still half-convinced that she'd been in his room last night.

"She's just—she's not a stranger, Jenna." His cheeks flushed.

"Not a stranger. That's the best you can do?" I grunted and stared ahead at the dark road. Hell, maybe he *did* like her. Maybe that was all this was about. My brother had the hots for Amber Velasco, EMT/narc/stalker. He was just too shy and backward to tell her, so he settled for making out (or close enough) with Queen Bitch Lanie Phelps instead. Of course, that didn't explain why Lanie Phelps wanted to make out with *him,* but maybe when your ex almost dies it kicks up weird hormones. "Who is she?" I asked for what felt like the millionth time. "Who?"

"You sound like an owl," my brother said. "Let it alone."

I pouted for the rest of the ride. Casey pretended to focus on driving: sensible, seeing as we'd nearly been killed in a car not that long ago. But I caught him glancing at me now and then out of the corner of his eye. At a stoplight, he rested his hand on my shoulder. That peaceful feeling seeped through me again.

Before it could take hold, I shrugged him away. "We promised each other," I snapped. "Remember?"

He didn't answer. I knew *he* knew that I was moving into territory that we never talked about, because talking about it made our family issues real, something that we tried to avoid at all costs.

"Remember, Casey?" I pressed in spite of myself, in spite of wanting that hand on my shoulder. "When you told me that Dad wasn't coming back. You said that Mom could never bring herself to tell us what we deserved to know. You said no secrets after that. Not between you and me. You said

we had to count on each other, remember? So what? That was just a lie?"

My brother's hands tightened noticeably on the steering wheel. "Not a lie," he said quietly. "Jenna, I—I can't . . . "

But by then we were at Mario's. He never did finish the sentence.

AMBER STOOD BEHIND the bar, drying off some beer glasses.

"What's been going on?" She eyeballed my brother like she knew he'd been up to something he shouldn't have been.

"Worked my shift," Casey answered tersely. "Now we're here. You heard anything about the blood work?"

"Did something else happen?" she asked.

He shook his head, but he shifted guiltily on his feet. He hadn't gotten stoned again; I would have *smelled* that. A new possibility occurred to me. Maybe Amber was a spy for the CIA or some foreign country. A Russian spy ring had mistaken me for some child agent and had been poisoning me, and she had recruited my brother to help her get to the bottom of things. The chopped beef churned in my belly. Believing that a Russian spy ring found my brother a possible asset was, again, only *slightly* more implausible than the whole Lanie Phelps incident.

My brother excused himself to pee.

I leaned at the bar, glaring at the back of Amber's head as she scooped strawberries into the blender on the counter behind her.

"You need to keep your energy up," she said, still facing the other way. She peeled a banana and added that, too, along with some kind of fruity looking liquid and ice cubes and let the blender rip. Amber turned and gave a smile. "Everyone loves my strawberry-banana smoothies," she said over the whirring.

"You need to leave us alone," I told her in a cold voice. The barbeque gave another jolt in my intestines. I willed it to stay put.

"Jenna—"

"I mean it. Leave me and Casey and our mom alone. I know you helped save me, but you're done now. Whatever it is you want from my brother, you need to forget about it. Casey may not be on to you, but I am."

I leaned into the bar, bringing my face close. I was not afraid of Amber Velasco. I wasn't even afraid of whoever had been coming into my room when I wasn't in my boots and sabotaging them. Which probably was her? But why? Because she knew I'd stand in the way of whatever was going on with her and my brother? Amber didn't stop smiling. Instead, she flicked off the blender, poured the smoothie into a to-go cup and handed it to me.

"Don't worry," she said. "Not spiked."

"No worries," I said.' "'Cause I'm not drinking it."

"I'm not your enemy, Jenna," she said cryptically.

"You're not my friend."

She turned and dumped more fruit and ice in the blender. Slapped the lid in place and pressed the button. Then she turned back. The blender whirred. So did my insides.

"Jenna," Amber said slowly, drawing out my name so that my skin prickled. Mario's was dark and quiet, but there was a glow over the bar. They must have had installed some kind of fancy recessed lighting to set a mood. "Your brother needs to—" She suddenly stopped mid-sentence and vaulted over the bar like an Olympic athlete.

I had to grab the smoothie to keep it from toppling, not

that I cared. She hightailed it over to my brother, now back from the john, lurking by the food pick-up window, and whispering into his cell phone. I could tell from his smile he wasn't talking to Dave.

Amber snatched the cell phone out of his hand and shoved it forcefully into his pocket. "Isn't it bad enough that I have to live here where people think Olive Garden is fine dining?" she hissed, loud enough for me to hear. "What do you think the AIC is going to say? Forget about your freaking ex-girl-friend! Glitches like these don't happen. It was supposed to be ten years from now, you know. At Austin Comic-Con. You were going to get smacked on the head with a model of the Millennium Falcon."

I gaped, slack-jawed at them. I supposed I was learning vital information. But it was gibberish.

Amber dragged Casey to the bar and plopped him down on the seat beside me. "Sit," she ordered. "Stay."

"What's the AIC?" I demanded. My brain was already a jumble of possible word combinations. *American Institute of Crime. Austin Investigation Council.* (She had mentioned Austin. And Comic-Con. *Austin Imposters at Comic-Con.*) Was there a synonym for narc that began with A?

Not surprisingly, Amber ignored the question. She poured a second smoothie into another to-go cup and handed it to me. It smelled different than mine, more medicine-y. "Give this to your mother. I added supplements for her electrolytes. And you need to drink yours. Now."

"I don't think so," I said to both demands. I turned to Casey.

He was ignoring me, too. For the first time since the acci-dent, he looked pissed. "What the hell do you expect, Amber? I never asked . . . Lanie never understood what happened to me. Why couldn't you have been here five years ago? That would have made sense. Five years ago and Jenna and my mother wouldn't have had to—"

"Because five years ago I was living with my boyfriend in Austin and going to UT. I was majoring in pre-med." Amber snapped her mouth shut. Slammed a fist on the bar. The entire room seemed to shake, even the barstools. "Go home, Casey. Take Jenna with you. We'll talk about this later."

Casey's glittering eyes smoldered. Still, he did not utter a word of protest. He grabbed the smoothies and stomped off to the door. Yes, I was happy to get the hell out of there. But part of me wanted to stay a little longer. See if she went ballistic again.

My stomach knot was back, tighter than ever.

I realized something then. Even when I'd been dying full time, I hadn't been truly afraid.

FOR PART OF the ride, Casey and I argued about the smoothies. Well, at least until I took a sip and found myself downing the whole cup. Amber Velasco may have been an increasingly terrifying creeper woman of mystery, but she made a damn good smoothie. The freaking thing tasted great. More than great. It soothed my dry throat. And even though I was angry and edgy and scared and confused, my head felt clearer than it had in months. I made a mental note to put more fruit in my diet. Fruit was cheap, at least.

"She's crazy," I said when I finished.

Casey shook his head. "No, she's not."

"Well, answer me this simple question. If she was premed five years ago, then why isn't she a doctor now? Why is she just an EMT?"

"She—it's okay, Jenna. I can't—damn it. Jenna." He

trailed off, sputtering. And thus ended the car ride portion of the conversation.

AT HOME, I stood by Mom's bed with Casey while she sipped the other smoothie.

"This is delicious," she said. She sounded lucid. She smiled at us over the to-go cup. She almost looked *healthy*. I glanced at the lamp on her nightstand. Whatever light bulb was in there, it was casting a particularly nice glow on her face. I peeked under the shade. It wasn't even one of the new environmentally sound ones. Just an old 75 watt.

Casey kissed Mom on the forehead. "Go to sleep," he told her. His voice sounded thick, as if maybe he wanted to cry. Not that I could blame him. A lump had formed in my own throat. *Just stay this way, Mom, please,* I begged. He clicked off the lamp and we stood in the dark until we were sure she had fallen asleep. I turned to him. There was nobody there. He'd already vanished into his room and shut the door. *Jerk*.

But: I noticed he'd left his phone on the front hall table. I scrolled through his contacts. Pressed Amber's number, which he had listed as Amber V. No answer. No voicemail. I needed to Google her, I decided. See if she had a Facebook page maybe. Someone had to know something about Amber Velasco. Even if it meant putting on gloves so I could use Casey's laptop without worrying about health hazards.

After that, I took a shower, changed into shorts and a T-shirt, stuffed the offending clogs under my bed—and did what I'd wanted to do since I'd been dragged from Ima Hogg. I called Mags.

"Casey?" she answered, sounding way too excited.

"No, it's his little sister. You know, your friend, Jenna?"

"Oh! Jeez. My bad. Sorry. It's just the caller ID—"

"I'm borrowing his phone. Listen, they figured out what was making me sick." I decided not to use the word poison. No use panicking my best friend. "Doc Renfroe says I'm going to be okay."

"That Amber person still around?" she asked. For the first time all day, I smiled, as in actually *smiled*. Mags was no slouch in the brain department. She knew there was something fishy.

"Yeah. And things have gotten a whole lot weirder, if you can believe it."

"I got your back, you know," Mags said.

I did know. I just didn't know if that would help.

CASEY HAD BEEN blasting some godforsaken punk rock band (at least an improvement over Katy Perry) when I finally mustered the energy to confront him with the handy excuse of returning his phone. I tapped on his door. No answer. I guess he was tired of arguing with me. His problem. I wasn't letting him off the hook anymore. Our life was messed up enough without adding a stranger and her secrets. Even Casey had to understand that.

I banged a little more loudly. I really didn't want to walk in there to find him with his laptop, or worse. On the third no-answer knock, I took a deep breath, turned the doorknob, and poked my head in.

"Casey?" I whispered.

He was standing twisted at the mirror, his shirt off, eyeballing his back. On each of his shoulder blades sat a dark nub, both about the size of my thumbnail. I watched as he poked one with his finger. I edged inside the room, too startled to make a peep. Something was sticking out of each nub.

Something that looked like . . . a feather? For a second, I thought I might be sick again. My brother had feathers growing out of his back? What the hell? Was somebody poisoning him, too?

Casey caught a glimpse of me in the mirror. He whirled around, eyes frantic. "Shit! Jenna. Get out!"

"No." I stood firm, his phone clutched in my hand.

"I'm serious!" he hollered. "I don't have a shirt on."

Like I hadn't seen that before? I walked to his bed, tossed the phone on his pillow, and picked up his T-shirt. "Here," I said, waving it in his face. "Problem solved."

His back was to the mirror now. My pulse quickened. "What is on your back?" I asked point-blank.

Casey snatched the shirt from me and started yanking (or trying to yank) it over his head. His hands were shaking. "Go back to your room," he growled, his voice muffled by the fabric. *Screw it.* I changed my mind midstream. I whipped the shirt off him before he could get his arms through the sleeves.

"Jesus!" my brother yelped. "What are you doing?"

I pointed to the feathers. That's what they were for sure. Feathers.

"So what did you do?" I said. "Get those at Spencer's? Did Bryce convince you to go there again?"

Casey's voice sounded sort of strangled. "No," he managed. "Shit. Jenna. You should sit down. I need to tell you something. About me. About Amber, too. Just give me the goddamned shirt, okay?"

More weirdness. (As in, weirdness inside.) Because as I handed him the shirt and sat on the bed, I felt woozy, not relieved. If I'd been scared before, then I was terrified now. For the first time, Casey himself looked stricken. He angled in the mirror again, eyeballing the nubs. "They're really there, aren't they?" he whispered.

"What's it got to do with Amber? You didn't get her pregnant or something did you?" Granted, that was the first time this thought had occurred to me, but I figured I needed to toss it out there. Maybe he'd done it with her. Maybe the thing on his back was some kind of sex disease. It wasn't like Ima Hogg went out of its way to educate us impressionable eighth grade youth about STDs. Maybe back feathers were common.

"No!" Casey gave a short laugh. "Is that what you think?"

"Is that what you did?" His laptop was open on the bedspread beside me and powered up. *Desperate times*, I thought. I pulled up Google. Typed in Amber Velasco.

"What are you doing?" he asked.

"I'm going to prove that she is up to no good. Someone has to know something about her. It has to be somewhere on the Internet."

He sighed. "She's not there. Believe me, I've looked." He moved from the mirror, rubbing at his left shoulder blade with his right hand. "There's three Amber Velascos but none of 'em are her. Trust me on that. I guess they wipe you clean if . . ."

I stood up. Before he could flinch or jerk away, I pressed one of the nubs. It felt hard and smooth. Spencer's made some quality products. Right? So why did I still feel scared? Because he didn't even blink?

"I need to try something," Casey said. "Stay there. Keep looking at my back, okay? Please, Jenna."

He squeezed his arms against his sides and made a grunting noise. Honestly, it sounded like he was trying to poop.

Against my better judgment, I stood still. The dark little nubs pushed forward from Casey's back. The feathers fanned out. Into tiny little damp wings. Like the kind of wings you see when a bird first hatches.

"You and Bryce need to stop wasting your money on all that comic book and video game crap," I said. My voice sounded funny in my ears, like I was listening to someone else talk. My gaze kept flickering over the feathers, hunting for any hint that they were fake. I'd never seen feathers so real, except on a bird. (Specifically on the pigeons that loitered outside the Ima Hogg dumpsters.) That sheen. It could be a flat monotone one moment, the glimpse of a prism the next. As if each feather were made up of shimmering little strands, thinner than human hair. Rippling like water when he moved even the slightest bit. "What are those, anyway? Something from a character in World of Warcraft?"

I clung to this last desperate hope for sanity. After all, Amber had mentioned Comic-Con in her nonsensical rant. Last year, Bryce had gone to Comic-Con in Dallas. I knew he was trying to convince Casey to go with him to the next one. Maybe this was Casey's costume. Now that my brother suddenly looked healthier than he had since football (or really ever), it was conceivable that he would want to go shirtless in front of the comic book community and try to bag Wonder Woman or something.

Casey squeezed again and grunted. The damp wings retracted. The nubs, too. They flattened against his skin.

"I don't understand," I squeaked. Maybe the antivenin had stopped working. Maybe I *wasn't* being poisoned. Maybe my not-Ebola was back. I was hallucinating. But why would I hallucinate *that*?

"I was dead," my brother said. "But they sent me back."

Full-fledged panic finally bloomed—a hard heart thump—in my chest. "Dead?"

"From the accident, Jenna. I died. You didn't. They sent me back."

Okay. He was crazy, too. Maybe it was safest to humor him. "Who sent you back?"

"I'm not sure. I couldn't see much, and they weren't big on introductions."

"You were in Heaven?" That's what he seemed to be saying. A piece of my brain began plotting my exit strategy. I would distract him, run from the room and call Dr. Renfroe. He could diagnose my brother's mental illness.

"No." Casey shook his head. "Not exactly. It was too dark to see where I was. They said I was a special case."

I glanced at the laptop still lying on his bed.

"They said I had to find out what really happened to Dad. What's going on with Mom. Why you've been so sick. We've sort of figured out that last one now, but we still need to find out who poisoned you." He sounded like he was checking off items on a list. He sounded the way he used to sound when he blew off homework until the last second. My mouth was hanging open. I closed it. "That's the deal. They said I had more to do with my life. They said I had to guard you. And only I could do it. Jenna, you have to understand, I could only hear voices, and it was pitch dark. But they sounded pissed. You know, with me in general. The weed and hanging out with Dave, mostly. Although the Prius scored some points. Especially since I'm from Texas."

I snorted, but began to relax. I decided to go along with his madness, just for the moment. I'd get in touch with Dr. Renfroe later. Better to document as much symptomatic behavior as possible. Anyway, I was insulted. Leave it to my

brother to come up with a delusion that makes Casey Samuels the hero. Yes, I'm a big enough loser to get stuck with *him*
as my guardian angel.

"So about Amber . . . she's an angel, too," he explained,
still sounding anxious. "I—She's, like, my boss. Well not
exactly, but she'll explain it to you now that you know.
She's probably gonna be pretty pissed I told you so soon. But
shit. I really couldn't keep it from you much longer, right?"
His voice abruptly became low and urgent. "You can't tell
anybody, though. That's part of it, too. We can't let anyone
know. Not Mom, not Mags, not a single living soul."

I tried to laugh. It came out more a gurgle. "Like I'd tell
anyone about this. You need help, Casey."

He looked directly into my eyes. For a second I felt dizzy.
"That's right, Jenna. I do need help. Your help. You don't
believe me, do you?"

"No." My heart rattled, threatening to bust out of my
ribcage. "No," I said again. "Stop it, okay?" Why was he
doing this? Had Dave hooked him up with something else
besides weed? The stoner stuff always felt harmless. But there
was more Dave sold, I knew. "Stop it. Stop it—"

"It's the truth," Casey interrupted.

Now I wasn't just frightened; I was angry. "No, it's not.
Do you think this is funny, Casey? 'Cause I don't. I just lost
my boots, someone is trying to kill me, and Mom is getting
worse. I don't have time for jokes. This is just plain mean."

Casey huffed out a breath. Unlike the foul norm, his
breath did not reek of tacos and corn nuts. It was totally
inoffensive. Not even the way neutral or minty breath (extra-
minty after weed) can be. It was pleasant. It was a puff of
fresh air. My heart gave another flutter.

"Jenna," he said quietly. "Think about it."

"No."

I thought about it anyway. My brain was not being obe-dient. The accident. The light. My brother's new hot bod. How Lanie was suddenly back in his life with no explana-tion. The Amber weirdness. The extra blood test that she had insisted upon. I thought about all of it. But no. There was just no way. Not here. Not *him*.

"Prove it," I said.

"Really?"

"Casey. Put yourself in my shoes." (Not that I had suit-able shoes anymore, but that was another story.)

"I wouldn't believe me, either," he mumbled. "Which is really sad, you know. Just hang on a second."

Now my pulse was dancing hip-hop.

Casey closed his eyes. "This takes a minute. I'm still get-ting used to it. Amber says it won't be long. Maybe another couple of days. She says newbies adjust pretty quick once they accept what's happened."

It was those last three words that got me. Because the only way someone becomes an A-word (not that this was what I believed) was by dying. My throat knotted up. No. No way was I going to accept that my brother was dead. Stoned, insane, tricked out with some weird costume—fine. But not dead.

Casey turned to face me, but I could see the nubs in the mirror. The room got brighter. Then brighter still. Casey's face lit up and then the glow extended to the rest of him. The nubs popped out. The feathers spread, bigger than before, still damp and unformed . . . but there was no denying it. Wings. He had wings. He was glowing, and he had wings. And I knew then they were nothing any high-end comic geek store could have ever possibly manufactured, because

costumes don't come with feelings you can beam to other people. They don't come with an invisible dose of bedazzled rapturous peace you can sprinkle on a spectator, when what that spectator really should do is scream and run for her life.

Holy shit. *Holy mother-loving crap.*

Casey wasn't lying. It was the truth. Just like he'd said.

Jenna's Journal

December 8th
JUST AFTER MIDNIGHT

S till, just in case, I came up with a series of questions. This was, after all, my only brother. It never hurt to double check.

The A-Word Test

(Note: I am not ready to say "angel" out loud. This is my compromise to myself.)

1) Does potential A-word have wing nubs on his back? Can he manipulate them to pop out and pop back in? (Poop noise optional.)

2) Did he go to the light? Can he prove it?

3) Can he do things that only an A could do?

4) If your brother suddenly looks a lot less geeky, and he has not had some TV show makeover, try re-geeking his appearance and see what happens.

5) Are girls—including the utterly inappropriate (one's best friend), the utterly impossible (the Heinous Ex), and the utterly creepy (whatever Amber proved to be)—now throwing themselves at his formerly stinky feet? Or close enough?

OBVIOUSLY, IF YOUR sibling is female, you would have to adjust accordingly—at least in the pronoun department. Also, if your sibling has never been a geek and (in spite of a fleeting romance with a cheerleader) has never secretly lusted after a life-size cardboard cutout of the entire cast of *Dr. Who*, you would have to substitute something more fitting.

I had other questions, but it was getting late. Besides, I was feeling weak again, although I wasn't sure if it was from the poison or the shock.

"All right," I said, pen in hand, test sheet on my lap. "Let's do this."

I'd returned to Casey's room after I'd finally stopped hyperventilating. If my test worked and showed that Casey really was an A-word now, then maybe I could trademark and patent the thing and sell copies on eBay. For all I knew, this happened a lot, and people just kept it quiet, which made total sense. It wasn't like I heard people talking in the Ima Hogg halls about how their Uncle Louie stroked out and then came back with wings. Nobody wanted to be labeled a nutcase. Mom couldn't even admit she was depressed.

"We don't really need to do this, Jenna."

"Yes, we do."

We started at the top. First, I inspected the wing nubs. He popped them out and opened the damp feathery clump and then wiggled his shoulders (a vast improvement over the constipated noise). Then he popped them back in. Just like before.

Wings: check.

"How come they're so, um, tiny?" I asked. Maybe they were like baby teeth; the first ones fell out and then the real ones grew in.

Casey scrunched his forehead. "New, I guess. I haven't really done much yet."

"Is that how it works? You have to earn bigger ones?"

He shrugged. "Don't know. Amber says I need to leave 'em alone until I'm not so new anymore. Seems kind of a waste to me, though."

"Lot of damn rules," I told him. "If she's telling you the truth." I was now so confused about Amber Velasco that my brain felt like it was going to explode from my skull and orbit into space. We'd worry about her later.

Casey began pulling his shirt back over his head.

"Keep it off," I ordered, and decided to jump to number four. I eyeballed his general physical appearance. Perfect wavy chestnut brown hair? Check. Six pack? Check. Defined arm muscles? Double check: one for each bicep. Superhero posture? Check.

My brother peered at himself, jabbed his forefinger against his now flat belly. His stomach—which before the accident had rested unceremoniously under his shirt like a poofy marshmallow—was now so rock hard that his fingertip actually bent. He flexed a toned arm and the bicep obediently showed its definition.

"I look hot," he remarked, sounding half giddy, half scared.

"Gross. Aren't angels supposed to be all holy?" The A-word had popped out of my mouth before I'd even realized it. But it was there, so I guess that meant I'd taken another small step towards accepting the unacceptable. I scribbled a number six on my list: *Is your brother now acting like an egotistical jerk?*

"Amber says it's something about the transformation process. I'll learn how to tone it down when I need to," Casey explained. He sounded disappointed. Either that or he was talking out of his ass. Maybe angels could be liars, too. I rolled my eyes. Was this why Lanie liked him again? His looks? Or was it something more, like A-word pheromones or something?

"What we need to do," I told him, frowning, "is to try to make the hotness go away. Then we'll see what happens."

"But Amber—"

"Leave Amber out of this. This is between us. Amber could think you're the prince of Egypt for all I know. I'm your sister. I have to be sure." Really, I already was. Mostly. Casey had begun to freaking *glow* while we argued. Which would explain all the weird tricks of light I'd noticed around him and Amber. (Ah . . . question number seven: asked and answered.) But I was a Texas girl, stubborn through and through. Besides, I didn't exactly come from a family of Bible thumpers. I didn't know jack shit about angels. I'd have to start from scratch, which also meant he couldn't fool me by twisting anything I thought I'd learned.

"What are you going to do to?" He looked nervous again. I could tell he didn't want me messing with his new body bounty.

An idea flashed. "Stay put," I told him. "I'll be right back."

Quietly, I tiptoed down the stairs and poked my head into Mom's room. She was curled in her comforter, snoring lightly. The empty smoothie cup still sat on her nightstand. She didn't even stir as I snuck by the bed and made my way

into the master bath. I closed the door before I turned on the light. *Sheesh*.

The bathroom was a pit. I couldn't remember the last time I'd dragged myself in there to clean. Now that I was on the mend, I needed to get after it. The towel over her shower stall stank of mildew. A ring of black mold dotted the drain of her sink. The contents of her makeup bag were strewn all over the counter. I guess it had taken her awhile to find that eye shadow she'd swiped on her lids the other day. Various items of clothing—none of which I'd seen her wear in forever—littered the floor of her closet.

I opened the cabinet under the sink. The mildew smell was making me queasy and I wanted my chopped beef and smoothie to stay put. I worked quickly, grabbing the various boxes of Lady Clairol she had stashed under there. Before my mother had given up on all things living, she'd been meticulous about her hair. In between salon highlights, she'd always made sure to do a little touch up. Now, of course, her hair had settled into a mousey brown with strands of gray.

She rolled onto her back as I walked by the bed again, the pile of coloring products clutched to my chest. I held my breath, then exhaled as she resumed snoring. I tiptoed out and back upstairs.

Casey was lying on his bed, scrolling through something on the laptop.

"Are you kidding me?" I dumped my haul at his feet.

He jolted guiltily and sat up. I peered at the screen. The page read, *Guardian Angel FAQ*.

"You Googled angels?" I guess it was better than what I thought he was doing. But not by much. If angels had to get their information from Wikipedia, no wonder the world was such a mess.

He reddened. "I wanted to look up some stuff. It's not like they gave me a manual. I thought maybe I'd do better if I studied the rules. The AIC doesn't make things easy, you know—"

"The AIC?" I interrupted. "That's what Amber was babbling about."

"Angels In Charge."

I actually laughed. "You're kidding, right?"

"Nope." He shook his head. "I'm already kind of a thorn in their sides. See, they weren't exactly expecting me this soon. But somehow they got me."

Somehow. I swallowed. Translation: He had died in a car wreck trying to save my life. He'd died prematurely. I shoved the thought from my brain.

"Get a towel," I said. "This might get a little messy."

Casey noticed the pile of hair color boxes. "What the hell is all that?"

"Well, I can't make your muscles go away. This is the only thing I can think of."

I explained my plan while I dragged him into our bathroom. Casey expressed his resistance. He really was an angel, he insisted. This whole checklist was a bunch of BS that I was using to deny the truth. Still, he surrendered, letting me snip off a bunch of his perfect waves: not enough to make him bald or anything, although it was tempting. I realized he was probably as curious as I was. I glopped Champagne Blonde on his head, brushing it over the spots I'd trimmed. The hair sucked up the color immediately—a small patch of Ken doll blond in the middle of the dark, shiny hair he'd been sporting since the accident.

I covered his head with the towel.

"How long?" he asked.

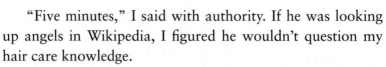

"Five minutes," I said with authority. If he was looking up angels in Wikipedia, I figured he wouldn't question my hair care knowledge.

Casey nodded. Those people up in Heaven must be having a good laugh right now. Or else their candidate pool had dwindled to the point of no return. If the best they could come up with was "Angels In Charge," I'd question their hiring practices, too. I moved us on to number three while we sat on Casey's bed and waited for the hair dye to maybe or maybe not disappear. As for number five, well, that one wasn't rocket science. Though it wasn't fair to Mags, Lanie was the prime offender. I assumed this had more to do with potential A-word status than with his natural personality or lack thereof.

Suddenly I felt bad. My stomach twisted. The chopped beef wasn't helping much, either. (I should have tried something smaller first. Maybe just the fries.) The Lanie thing wasn't fair to *him*, either. He'd completely given up on taking care of himself when she'd dumped him. Even a shallow twit like Lanie deserved a second chance, though, right? Unless she wasn't a shallow twit at all? Unless she'd grown up enough to apologize and forgive him? Still, what did a second chance even mean? What if Lanie *was* back in his life only because Casey was now the thing I didn't want to say? It probably meant they were even more doomed as a couple.

Now I was cranky again. I shook it off. Marched us forward on the list. "Do something angel-y," I said, trying once more to sound authoritative.

"Like what? That Wikipedia page was pretty vague."

"Well," I said, thinking hard. "If you're really an angel, then you probably can't be hurt, right?"

Casey's gaze strayed to the bong sitting on the floor by his dresser.

"Stay focused," I told him. He'd told me himself that marijuana was frowned upon by the AIC. I rose from the bed and grabbed the scissors from the bathroom. The ends were rounded and dull, but the edge had some sharpness. It would have to do. I didn't give Casey time to argue—just reached over quickly and sawed the edge of the scissors against his right bicep.

"Hey!" He stepped back, his foot grazing the bong. It teetered, stray droplets of the stinky brown water sloshing over the rim. "What the hell, Jenna?" A thin drizzle of blood trickled down his arm.

"Don't wipe it off," I commanded. "We need to wait."

We watched his bicep and waited. So: angels could bleed like regular people. Maybe it was that transition thing. I glanced up at his eyes, and then back at his arm. My breath caught in my throat. The cut had vanished. Just like that. His skin was smooth and unblemished. No sign of blood. Nothing.

"Whoa," Casey said. He sounded stoned. I couldn't blame him. *Check.*

The five minutes was up. Back in the bathroom, we faced the mirror. Carefully, I unwound the towel from his head.

"Crazy!" Casey smoothed his perfectly wavy and definitely *not* Clairol Champagne Blonde hair. I had tried to change him. I had failed.

Check.

"What about number five? I could call Lanie." Casey looked at me hopefully.

I would have kicked some sense into him, but my boots were gone and no way was I putting those purple clogs back

on. There was nothing left but number two. We both knew it. (Maybe before I patented the A-Word Test, I'd shuffle the order so that The Question of Questions wouldn't be saddled with the unfortunate poop association of #2.) My brother's expression grew serious. He pressed a hand to my cheek. In the mirror, I noticed that his nails were neatly filed and buffed to a male-model sheen.

"Enough," he said. "I died, Jenna. I know you don't want it to be true. But I really did." Again, with his skin against mine, I felt that familiar wave wash the fear and confusion away. But I fought to cling to the uncertainty. I didn't *want* to be certain. I wanted Casey Samuels, perv stoner. It seemed as if he had a bunch more to say. But all that came out was, "I'm sorry. I've been a crappy brother."

I shook my head. "You're not," I choked out. Bad taste in girlfriends, yes. Crappy, no.

"I am. Shit, Jenna. Look at me. I was failing Teen Leadership class, Jenna. No one fails Teen Leadership."

I laughed. I sniffed and blinked. A big fat tear dripped down my cheek. It glistened a little in Casey's residual glow. There was one thing I hadn't added to the list: *Did the A-word die trying to save you?* My brother had died trying to get me to the hospital. We could pretty it up any way we wanted, but those were the facts. Casey had died in the accident. I had lived.

"I'm sorry you're dead," I whispered.

Casey pulled me into a hug. "Me, too."

We stood hanging onto each other, that new nice smell of his floating up my nostrils. I believed him now. And yes, there was something about his hugging me that buried the sadness. Only this time I didn't try to fight it. I guess that was the angel part. I guess that's what they did.

"You really can't tell Mom, Jenna," he said. "Or Dad if we find him. You need to promise."

"I promise. I just . . ."

"What?"

"Nothing." I stepped back from him. But I wanted to ask: Why me? Why was it okay to tell *me*? I didn't know if I was ready to hear that answer. Plus I wasn't sure if he even knew the answer. But I bet Amber did. I'd hear the rest of it soon enough. I yawned. We both had school tomorrow. Today, I guess, since it was after midnight. "Do you still have to go to school and work?" I asked.

How sweet would that be? Maybe he could do something about the detention I hadn't served. This whole angel thing might have its advantages.

"Yeah," Casey said. "I mean I still have to work to support us. That's part of the deal with me coming back. And Amber says I have to go to school, too. That way people won't get suspicious. I need to keep up appearances while I figure everything out. Besides, who else could Bryce count on for the dinner shift?"

"Bryce is a pissant," I stated.

I yawned again, too exhausted and emotionally drained to ponder Amber's role in all this. At least for tonight. Could I trust her now? I didn't know. When was she going to tell Casey all the stuff he needed to know? Or had she, and was he just covering it up so he wouldn't scare me? It had been just Casey and me for so long. Now there was Amber, who it seemed wasn't going away anytime soon. But that didn't mean that she was completely honest or good-hearted, did it? After all, Casey still seemed perfectly capable of BS. Nor did it mean that any of this was a good thing.

"Maybe people will tip bigger at BJ's," I said, my brain racing. "Maybe you can make 'em."

Casey grinned. "Maybe."

There were probably a lot of angel angles to work. Okay. Time to go to bed. My brother might be my guardian now, but I still had to keep my eyes open. Somebody had tried to poison me. I wasn't dying anymore, at least not that I knew. But I wasn't safe. Especially since my *brother* had apparently been assigned to figure this whole mess out. Okay, that sounded meaner than I meant, but Casey was never a deep thinker. He was an instinct guy. *Make out with Lanie! Get stoned! Risk everything to drive little sister to the hospital!* If the A-word transition process was a long one, I probably couldn't afford to wait.

Jenna's Journal

December 8ᵗʰ
LATER THAT MORNING

In the morning, I checked on Mom. She ate some toast in bed. I brewed her a pot of coffee and made her swallow a vitamin. I had to hold the glass while she drank. Her muscles seemed extra weak today, or maybe I was just noticing because I was feeling stronger. Then I helped her into a clean pair of sweats, and she held her arms up so I could slip a gray tank top over her head. I wanted to put her into a T-shirt, but everything she owned was dirty. I needed to get after the laundry.

Then I got myself dressed for school.

Here is what I wore: jeans, a purple tank top and my gray hoodie with the plaid lining. Also my old gray Converse with the black laces. I double-checked them. As far as I could tell, they were poison-free. But they were not my boots. My poor Ariats that I would never wear again! My feet were still itchy, by the way, and I was on and off thirsty, but I figured I'd keep popping the Cipro and things would get better. When I came back to say good-bye to Mom, she was still chewing the same piece of toast, staring off into nowhere.

Here is the stupid thing I did then: I started to cry. My eyes filled with tears. My throat plugged up. I looked away when she asked me what was wrong.

"Nothing," I croaked.

I had assured Casey that I wouldn't tell her about what had happened to him, and I aimed to keep that promise. But for a few rotten seconds, it seemed horrible and unfair.

Then I looked up. Casey had appeared behind me in Mom's doorway. He reached over his shoulder and scratched a spot on his back, right where I knew those wing nubs sat.

"You look really handsome, sweetheart," my mother told him.

She was right. He did. He stood tall and arrow-straight, eyes sparkling. I was happy beyond words that he looked so good. I was sad beyond words because I knew why. Sadder when I looked at Mom. At how she was. And because she had no idea why Casey was all shiny and new.

"I have to brush my teeth," I said, bolting before I lost it completely. In the bathroom, I splashed water on my face and blew my nose. I frowned at my puffy red eyes and splotchy face. Then I overheard Mom's voice.

"Why is Jenna so sad?" she was asking Casey.

I decided to skip saying good-bye to her on the way out.

THE GILROYS WERE hanging up their Christmas lights when we locked up the house and climbed into the Merc. Mr. Gilroy, dressed in Dickies overalls and a tan Henley shirt, was perched on a ladder, screwing in bulbs. I saw that they had already decorated the yard with a manger scene and two

lit-up full-sized angels. Maybe once they got them plugged in, Casey could go stand in the middle.

Mrs. Gilroy hot-footed it across the strip of grass between our houses, a tangled extension cord clutched in her hands. "That looks like Nell Pittman's car," she observed. She wore black velour pants and a button-down red Christmas sweater with Santa heads all over it. A white pom-pom sat at the top of each Santa hat.

I shut the passenger side door on her and leaned out the window. "Manger's looking good," I said. "Y'all get rid of the reindeer?"

I knew they had. Last Christmas Brett Colson and some of the other Spring Creek football guys had driven around the neighborhood in the middle of the night for two weeks straight moving everybody's reindeer into compromising positions. Mrs. Gilroy had never gotten over the shock of walking down the driveway for her morning paper only to find Donner and Blitzen humping each other.

"The Prius is in the shop," Casey added. "This here's a loaner." As if to prove it, he shoved one of the leftover snickerdoodles into his mouth. (I didn't know if angels had to eat, but my brother had not lost his interest in chowing down.)

"Nell really doesn't mind y'all using her car?" Mrs. Gilroy asked.

Why the hell do you care? I wondered.

"Hmm," Casey said under his breath. He revved the engine. "Uh-oh. Looks like MJ's in trouble." He pointed to Mr. Gilroy, still at the top of the ladder. The strand of lights he'd just tacked up had come unpinned, dangling just out of his reach. Then he tore out of the driveway. "Best not to go overboard with this stuff," he muttered. "Mrs. Gilroy is too damn nosy."

"What stuff?" I asked him.

He hung a right at the Kroger center and parked by the doughnut shop.

Had he done something to make those lights dangle? I didn't mind if he had. Mrs. Gilroy *was* nosy. "Casey, what happened back there?" I persisted.

"Nothing. We're meeting Amber," Casey said without any other explanation.

Sure enough, Amber was inside by the window, dressed in her EMT outfit, munching on a sausage and cheese kolache. Snickerdoodles and now kolaches.

"Do y'all need to eat?" I asked as Casey and I plopped into two empty chairs at her little table.

"Jenna!" Casey scowled.

"Morning to you, too," Amber said. She made a point of biting into her kolache. Cheese oozed onto her lower lip and she dabbed it with a napkin. "And no. But I enjoy it. Some of us don't. My theory is they never liked food that much in the first place. I did. I still do. But if you want great kolaches, you really need to go to the Hill Country. There's this little doughnut shop outside of Fredericksburg that makes cheese and fruit kolaches to die for." She smiled. "Metaphorically speaking." She looked from me to Casey and then back to me. "I take it your brother has filled you in."

I couldn't even nod.

Casey bought himself a blueberry doughnut. Then we all headed outside where we could talk more privately. There was a bench a few stores down—in front of Texas Nail Salon, which didn't open until ten. We sat with our doughnuts. Well, *they* did. I'd lost my appetite.

The gist of the conversation was this: Of course Amber knew Casey had told me. That was Amber's job. The AIC

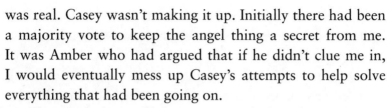

was real. Casey wasn't making it up. Initially there had been a majority vote to keep the angel thing a secret from me. It was Amber who had argued that if he didn't clue me in, I would eventually mess up Casey's attempts to help solve everything that had been going on.

The more I listened, the more pissed I became.

Who was running the show up there in angel land? The same people who believed that WWF was real wrestling? My brother had a 33 average in Teen Leadership, but *I* was untrustworthy? Casey would remain on a sort of probationary period for awhile. That was the only part that made sense. The results of Mom's blood work were still pending.

"But something's not right," Amber concluded. "My friend at the lab wants to run more tests."

I wondered if the AIC sat around playing cards or harps or whatever and decided, *Hey, I know what'll perk things right up. Let's screw with the Samuels family. It'll help pass eternity.* "Y'all are holy beings, right?" I wasn't quite sure if I could extend this to my brother, but I put it out there in general terms. "If you're angels doesn't that mean you just *know* stuff? Why does it all have to be a mystery? I mean, can't you just tell us who's been poisoning me and what's going on with Mom and what happened to Dad?"

Amber slurped another gulp of coffee from the Styrofoam cup. "No," she said slowly. "That's not how it works." She twitched her mouth. "When I'm—when we're like this," she motioned to herself and Casey, "we're bound by Earth rules. Human form. Human rules. There's a little more to it, but that's the basics."

I glared at her. "The basics?" My brother might have used his A-powers to mess with the neighbors' holiday décor. We needed the advanced course.

She met my gaze. "Think about it, Jenna. You wouldn't really want a world where everything was predetermined, would you? What fun would that be?"

Suddenly we were in a staring contest. I blinked first. Now I was cranky again. The guarantee of free will aside, I knew that Amber and the AIC were convinced that my father's disappearance was not just a random event, and that Dad was somehow tied into everything else, including my poisoned boots. Casey was back because he was best suited to connect the dots. But she was still lying to me. I was sure of it.

"Throw this stuff away, would you?" Amber pressed her napkin and empty Styrofoam cup into my brother's hands. Obediently, he trotted toward the garbage can. I stifled a grin. Okay, maybe she wasn't *evil*. It was sort of a kick to see someone bossing around my brother.

Plus honestly, she had told me stuff I'd wanted to know. I didn't like her any better, but I could tolerate her. For now, at least. For Casey's sake.

"They didn't want to send him back, Jenna," she whispered. "But someone, I can't say who, argued that your brother had potential."

"And you're telling me this because?"

Amber lowered her voice. On her utility belt, her cell phone gave a soft little beep. The red light started blinking. Someone needed her. I wondered if it was someone human. "Because I think you deserve to know. Because we all heard you praying for him in that car."

"I don't pray." This wasn't entirely true, but I felt like pissing her off. She still thought she knew me. She still absolutely did not.

"Things happen for a reason, Jenna."

More bullshit. Or maybe she'd read my mind. Maybe she

knew about Maggie's philosophy of life, too. I thought long-ingly about my boots.

"So what happened to *you*?" I asked. "How come you're an A-word? I figure it's only fair I know since you seem to know so much about *us*."

She blinked at me. For the first time ever, she was at a loss for words. I almost felt sorry for her. Almost. "It doesn't mat-ter," she muttered. "Listen, Jenna. I get it. I really do. You heard what I said last night; I know you did. Angels aren't always infallible. The world is set in motion and sometimes things happen. Scientists call it chaos theory; philosophers call it free will. My explanation? It's just the way Nature works."

Yes, I understand. Once again, you are telling me that (shit happens.) *You've just given it a fancier set of names.*

"Your brother's friend Dave is the type who brings extra chaos. It's like dominos, Jenna. Casey did something kind for his friend. He loaned him your car. But Dave's behavior while in the car . . . that was the wild card."

"Are you telling me that a bunch of advanced supernatu-ral beings couldn't predict that loaning a guy who smoked his breakfast—and lunch and dinner—was going to turn out badly?"

Amber opened her mouth, then closed it

Casey had paused by the garbage can. Then I saw why. He was chattering away on his cell phone again with that same dumb grin he'd worn last night with Lanie Phelps.

"Listen, you asked why I'm here," Amber whispered furiously. "There was this angel from A&M. We got into a little, um, debate about football. I mean, who doesn't believe that the Longhorns are the better team? Turns out there's a lot of Aggies after, you know. *After*. Who would have thought? They're a bunch of self-righteous sons of bitches, by the way."

I laughed in spite of myself. Okay. I may not have trusted her entirely yet, but I'd clearly underestimated this woman. Because finally, Amber Velasco had said something that made some sense. The A&M/UT rivalry was legendary. In Texas, almost everyone sided with either the Aggies or the Longhorns. Even when they weren't playing in the same conference. The Aggies weren't much for Austin, said it was filled with hippie-types and liberal tree-huggers. Longhorns dismissed College Station as a rinky-dink country town.

I was generally neutral about the whole thing, but my favorite asshat (or not), Mr. Collins was an Aggie through and through. I wouldn't have held this against him, but Aggies were sticklers for their football traditions and Collins had tried to put an Aggie guilt trip on my brother when he quit the Spring Creek team. "You were always there for me, Samuels," he'd growled. "Even if you weren't playing. You were my 12th Man. Now you're nothing."

Here's how the Aggie 12th Man thing worked: Only eleven guys went out on the field to play, but the whole student body was that twelfth. A win for the team was a win for everybody. You didn't leave in the middle. Of course it had never occurred to Mr. Collins to wonder if *he* was the one who was quitting on Casey. It sure as hell hadn't occurred to Lanie Phelps. Or had it, finally?

"You got stuck with my brother because you went to UT?" I managed.

It did sound like the lamest possible excuse. On the other hand, it was highly entertaining. But I still didn't know how she had died.

"Casey!" Amber hollered before I could ask any more

questions. "Stop acting like a jackass and take your sister to school!"

WE WERE PULLING up to Ima Hogg when Casey turned to me. His well-groomed brows pinched toward each other. He made a "hmm" sound. For a second, he looked kind of constipated.

"Casey," I warned. "You can't show your wings in the Ima Hogg driveway."

"What? No. I was just thinking."

"About what?"

"You."

This was not the answer I'd expected. I figured he was daydreaming about Lanie Phelps and how maybe they could do it in the locker room or something. (I meant no disrespect to either of them, but let's face it. I had recently heard Dave describe Casey's situation, in between bong hits, as such: *"You couldn't get laid if you were a load of cement."* Neither could Dave, but that wasn't the point. The point was that this was an accurate description of my brother until the day he died and came back like this. It took some getting used to.)

"What *about* me?" I rested my hand on the door. I needed to get to class. Someone behind us honked a horn. We were messing up the drop-off rhythm.

"Who would want to hurt you, Jenna? No one. You're a pain in the ass sometimes, but you're in the eighth grade. You're not exactly a threat to mankind. Who would want to hurt Mom? Same answer. She's not someone people hurt. She's Holly Samuels, a speech therapist at Oak View Convalescent Home. At least she was. And a mom. No one hurts someone like that. I mean, look at Dr. Renfroe. He still looks out for Mom and she doesn't even work for him anymore.

So here's what I'm thinking. Dad's disappearance must be connected somehow. You heard what Mom was saying. I know we both figured she was rambling nonsense, but what if she wasn't? What if Dad is alive? What if wherever he went or whatever happened to him is the same reason someone went after you? What if it's the same reason Mom's so wacked out? Like we were thinking—not just depressed, but something else, maybe."

Goosebumps rose on my arms. The Merc was still idling in the middle of the drop-off lane. More people had started honking. Out of the corner of my eye, I saw the school cop plodding toward us. (For the record: Officer Jenkins weighed in at about two-eighty. If we had a real emergency here at Ima Hogg, he would probably bust a clot before he actually caught up with anyone.) But Casey wasn't done. He rested a hand on my shoulder to calm me.

"Jenna, I keep going over and over what Mom said. Like, that he's been trying to contact her, but he has to stay hidden. What if all that's true? What if something's been keeping him away? What if he's *scared* to come back? So I asked myself: If a guy—if Dad—is totally terrified of something, what's the one thing you can threaten him with to make him do what you want? What would make him come back? Only one thing as I see it. Something that would make him even *more* terrified."

"Like what?" I asked.

"You," he said.

My heart was beating too fast for me to speak.

"What I mean is: Like someone he loves, in danger. Like someone trying to poison you. Think about it, Jenna. Maybe whoever poisoned you figured that if you got sick enough, it would make Dad come home to try to save you. Maybe they're

even trying to make Mom sick, too, for the same reason. Maybe they're trying to ambush Dad when he comes to save us all."

My goosebumps turned to boulders. Was this possible? I had convinced myself that our father didn't love us. That he'd run off to some new place or new life. In my worst moments, I sometimes even thought that it was partly because of me. I didn't know why, but it had to be something. Why else would he disappear after promising to ride Magic Mountain with me at Disney World?

Back then, Casey already played football. He had promise. Hard to believe, but he did. I was just a hyper nine-year-old who liked to come with her father when he scoped out the different restaurants to review. I liked going to the sports games, too, sitting with him in the press boxes at Minute Maid and Reliant and Toyota. But I loved the restaurants most of all. Casey never wanted to go, but I did. Dad would order brisket or ribs or—for the sequel he'd started on classic Tex Mex—street tacos and refried beans and fresh guacamole and enchiladas with gooey cheese and sauce. He'd share his plate with me and we'd confer. Were the ribs smoky enough? Was the brisket too fatty? How about that guacamole? Had the avocados been fresh?

It was just me and Dad and the three meat platter. Or Combination Number Two with an extra cup of queso because my father liked to dip his chips in the molten cheese. Or fresh salsa studded with jalapenos that made me sweat after the first bite . . . After five years without him, though, I had come to the conclusion that my memories were mistaken. My father hadn't enjoyed those times. I'd just "projected." Maybe I'd eaten too many enchiladas. Or given him a lousy opinion about the tacos al carbon.

I willed my heart to beat like a normal person's instead of

dancing in my chest like a lunatic. "You think that could be true?" I croaked.

"Yeah," he said. "I do."

Something inside me that had felt sad and broken knitted itself together just the tiniest bit. And Casey wasn't even touching me anymore.

Officer Jenkins tapped on my window. "Get a move on," he grumped through the glass.

"I'm gonna find him, Jenna," Casey whispered, opening the door for me. "I'm gonna bring him home."

"It's been five years, Casey."

"It's okay," my brother said. He lowered his voice. Officer Jenkins was right outside the Merc. "I'm a you-know-what now. That's how we roll."

"Don't ever say 'how we roll' again," I told him. "Or I'll report you to that AIC."

The bell rang. Nice. I was late for Algebra. Again.

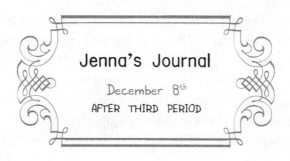

Jenna's Journal

December 8th
AFTER THIRD PERIOD

"How you doing today, Jenna?" Mr. Collins asked, pausing during aisle patrol while we were solving for x. "You had me worried."

"Doctor got me fixed up," I said. "Gave me a shot and everything."

Mr. Collins patted me on the shoulder. "Glad to hear it." He leaned down, treating me to his morning coffee breath. "I meant what I said yesterday. If you need something—if there's something I can help you with, I want you to ask." He sounded sincere. "And as long as you're all healthy now," he added, "I'll tell Mrs. Monahan to expect you at detention this afternoon. That'll take care of today's tardy as well. Call it my little gift."

Or maybe not so much.

"Dandy," I told him.

"That's the spirit." He straightened his A&M tie. *I bleed maroon*, he liked to tell us. Maroon and white were the A&M colors. I thought about Amber's grudge against the

Aggies. Maybe that Aggie angel had flummoxed her just like Mr. Collins was flummoxing me. But that was algebra; we were always looking for the unknown.

I guess I stared at his tie too long. He spouted off another A&M analogy. Mr. Collins was big on analogies. "You need to think like an Aggie, Jenna," he said. "If things don't go your way, you haven't lost. You've just run out of time. Next time you'll beat the hell outta your opponent."

I didn't want to think like an Aggie. Plus, part of the whole problem was that we didn't know who our opponent was.

MAGGIE GRABBED ME in the hall on the way to English. "You had me freaked!"

Today she had on a dark wash denim skirt, black fishnets, black ankle boots and her same hoodie covering a black leather bustier. This was a new look. Maggie was all about new looks. My legs were so pale that if I wore fishnets, people would think I was wearing black and white checked tights.

"I'm good," I told her. "Really."

"Truth?" She scanned me like she was looking for a clue.

I hooked pinkies with her. "Truth," I said. "My enzymes were messed up. They took some blood and found out what to give me to make it better."

"You're not wearing your boots," she said.

I sighed. "Nope. They were hurting my feet." This wasn't a lie. It also wasn't the whole story.

WE SCRIBBLED NOTES again in English.

Maggie: Is ur brother hooking up with Lanie Phelps again? That's what I heard.

Me: Maybe.

Maggie: Seriously?

Me: Maybe.

Maggie: Did u have doughnuts this morning? Bring me one?

Me: Yes. No. Sorry. How did u know?

Maggie: Caleb McIntyre saw you.

She leaned over to whisper. Mrs. Weiss was at her desk, and we were supposed to be drafting persuasive essays on the topic of our choice. Mine was *Should Public School be Mandatory?*

"Did you and Casey eat doughnuts with that Amber woman?"

"Um, yes?"

"You're not sure?"

"No. I mean, yes. She was at Sundale eating kolaches. I talked to her while Casey was . . . yeah. I saw her."

"She ate kolaches with Casey?" Maggie crossed her arm. She'd said Casey's name the way girls say the name of a boy they like.

I heaved a sigh. This female attraction thing to Casey 2.0, A-Word version, was getting old. Maggie did not like Casey. Maggie thought Casey was a weed-loving pissant. I changed the subject. "We're looking for my dad again. Casey thinks maybe we'll actually find him."

"Really?" Maggie's mouth formed a little O. "Why?"

I hadn't expected her to question our motives. But this was Mags. She was looking for signs. "Because Mom told us she's heard from him," I whispered. "I'll let you know what we find."

"Girls." Mrs. Weiss put her finger to her lips and motioned for us to get back to work.

"So that's it?" Maggie whispered as I turned back to my essay.

"Yeah. I'm not gonna get my hopes up." This too, was true.

"Maybe you should," Maggie said suddenly, loud enough that Mrs. Weiss gave us another dirty look.

"Why?"

"Hope's a good thing," Maggie said.

"So is doing your work," Mrs. Weiss added. "Which I *hope* will show your best effort."

I hated when teachers eavesdropped.

Maggie cast sideward glances at me until the bell rang.

"You can tell me, you know," she said as we pushed our way into the hall toward science. "Whatever it is. I'm your best friend, Jenna. It's my job description."

"I know," I said. But all the way to science, I wondered what it was going to be like having a secret that I had to keep forever.

H ow I Got Out of Detention. Again.

Casey's theory—that Mom was right, that Dad was on the run from something, that the bad guys who had him on the run wanted him to resurface, so they'd defiled my boots with poison—all of it circled my brain for the rest of the day like a toilet bowl on permanent flush.

Here are the questions that I came up with:

1) How could my mom be right about anything, given her condition? (Then again, given what had happened to Casey, I was in a better position to believe the farfetched.)

2) Speaking of Casey, why poison me and not my brother?

3) Where *was* Dad? Why did Mom think he was in Mexico?

4) Was there something about the last day we had seen Dad that might give us a clue? I had to trust Casey on this one. He

knew from the beginning that Dad hadn't come home that day. All I remember is that he and Mom kept telling me that Dad was on a business trip. Mom had insisted that she and Casey maintain this lie at my expense until she finally accepted that his disappearance was of the more permanent sort. At the time, their story seemed plausible. Dad was a sportswriter. Basketball season was in full swing and baseball had just begun. Usually, he covered home games, but it wasn't much of a stretch to believe that he was traveling with the Rockets and then the Astros. The problem was, I was already a good reader and one of my father's biggest fans. His columns were suddenly no-shows in the newspaper and online. Eventually, Mom and Casey had no choice but to tell me the truth.

5) What would happen if and when we solved this whole mess? Would Casey still be here? Or would he disappear, too? Probably best not to overthink that one. He was here now. Did he know I'd printed copies of Dad's columns from the online version of the *Chronicle*? I still kept this one folded up in my underwear drawer:

Timeless
By MIKE SAMUELS,
Houston Chronicle

A pal recently commented that he disliked baseball. Why? I asked him. "Too slow," he said. "No clock. How can you find it exciting if there's no clock? Where's the tension?"

I had no argument for the clock. Baseball takes as long as baseball takes. That's the beauty of it. The pleasure.

Football is a religion and basketball, a dance. But baseball's rhythms vary: the toe-tapping teeter of a runner readying to steal a base. The muscular flutter of a pitcher winding up to rocket the ball across the plate. The aerodynamic power of bat hitting ball. The aerobic stretch of the umpire signaling that the runner is safe. The surging dash of the outfielder racing for the ball and the ballet leap to snatch it from the air.

But, said my friend, annoyed, "That doesn't respond to my point. The game's not timed. How can you sit through that?"

"Come with me," I said. "next home game. See it through my eyes. Then you'll understand."

My father—who died of heart disease when I was a sophomore in college—took me to my first Astro's game. They played at the Dome then: the eighth wonder of the world, they called it. Since then I've come to understand that this was not the best place to play baseball. No option for open air, no real grass. But it was the game I savored, the time with my father, the conversation that baseball allows.

He taught me the game, my old man. First-base-side, as close to the field as possible. This is where he liked to sit. We'd crack open peanuts in the shell, chow down on hot dogs (two each, with mustard), sip Cokes and the game would unfold. No cheerleaders, no half time show. Just me, my father, and the game.

He taught me what the catcher's signs meant. He showed me how to watch for a runner getting ready to steal third or home. "Sort of like poker," he said. Every player has a tell—some sign that lets you know what he's up to. But only if you're watching closely.

He told me about the players and their stats. We filled out score cards—always in pencil. My father was old school; singles marked with a diagonal slash and 1B. We filled in players' names and numbers for their positions. Designated HR or FC for fielder's choice. Our cards told the story of the game. If the batter hit a grounder to the pitcher who fielded it and threw him out at first, we'd mark this in the shorthand my father taught me. We'd eat and drink and talk and analyze. Days later, months, weeks, years, I could re-read those score cards and remember the game. No video replays needed (cont.)

Note: there was another half a page to this article, but it had fallen out of my journal before I pasted everything tight. That part talked about Dad taking me and Casey with him and teaching us the same stuff. He did not mention that Casey had the same gripe that had inspired the article: the game was too damn slow. This was why Casey liked football. (Plus, he was a boy from Texas.) I was the one who was more like Dad in that regard. I liked a game where I didn't always have to pay absolute attention every second.

AT THE END of the day, I headed to Mrs. Monahan's room, prepared to gut it out with the other delinquents. Among them was Corey Chambers, who chose to flop into the seat next to me, possibly so my nasal passages could bask in the foul reek of his cigarette smoke.

"Anderson?" Mrs. Monahan began droning the attendance roster. I shuffled through my binder for my persuasive essay. Ah, detention: another example of how mandatory public school infringed upon our personal freedoms.

"Bates?"

Corey Chambers poked me in the arm. I ignored him. He poked again. Corey was as hard to get rid of as his fumes.

On the other side of me, Madison Riley elbowed me and giggled. (Madison appeared harmless, but she could pull hair like nobody's business—which she did on a regular basis if anyone looked sideways at her.) I looked up. My brother stood in the doorway of Mrs. Monahan's room, gesturing to me with his finger. Had he actually gone to school today? I guess it didn't really even matter, but this whole thing would be easier if we stuck to a plan. "When did your brother get so hot?" Madison asked. She was staring at Casey like she wanted to leap on him and wrap her skinny arms around his neck.

"Your brother's here," Corey said. Nobody at Ima Hogg had quite mastered the art of the obvious like Corey. He leaned closer and stage-whispered, "tell him to let Dave know I need to talk to him later. It's urgent, dude." Corey called everybody dude, regardless of gender. Even the teachers.

"Colvert?" Mrs. Monahan looked up and frowned.

Casey stepped into the room with a bright-toothed smile. "You are looking well today, Mrs. Monahan," he said politely. Mrs. Monahan had been Casey's social studies teacher when he was at Ima Hogg. She was one of those barrel-shaped people with all her weight in the middle and spindly legs that looked like they could barely support her. There was no way in this life or the next that she could look "well."

The other twenty-five juvenile offenders jerked their heads up in unison.

"Mr. Samuels, what are you doing here?" she demanded.

"I need Jenna," Casey said.

"Can I talk to Casey?" I was up and skidding to the door before Mrs. Monahan—who (naturally) seemed as dumbfounded as Madison by the new and improved Casey—could say no.

"Why are you here?" I whispered. Not that I didn't appreciate it, but if he actually did spring me from detention, I worried that people would start talking. I wanted to attract as little attention to myself as possible right now.

Behind me, I heard Madison giggle again. Perfect. Now there was no way that people *wouldn't* talk.

"Because I think I figured something out," Casey said. He shoved his hand in his pocket and pulled out a slip of paper.

It took me a few seconds to recognize what he was holding. After all, I hadn't looked at it since I shoved it into the kitchen junk drawer about two years ago. For three years before that, it had been stuck to the refrigerator with a Domino's Pizza magnet. Originally, my father's note had been up there, too. But after the millionth time I'd come into the kitchen and found my mother reading the note and crying, I'd ripped the note into pieces and thrown it into the garbage. Later, I discovered that Casey had pulled it out, taped it back together and hidden it in his sock drawer. Somehow the expired certificate for a fajita dinner for four from Manny's Tex Mex had escaped my wrath.

"Are you showing me this because you want fajitas?" I decided not to ask the obvious follow-up: Had he been smoking? Maybe angels didn't have to eat, but pot could still make him hungry. I eyeballed him. He didn't look high.

"I'll tell you in the car," Casey replied. He stepped back in the room. "It's an emergency," he said to Mrs. Monahan.

She hesitated, looking from Casey to me and then back to Casey, who turned on that high-wattage smile again. "Then you better go," she said to me.

I didn't have to be told twice. I rushed to grab my crap before Mrs. Monahan remembered that this was the Samuels family, for whom she did not have a great deal of affection.

"Couldn't you have at least have made her mark down I was there?" I huffed as Casey whisked me down the hall. "I'm going to have detention until the end of time."

"You know it doesn't work that way, Jenna."

"You sure? Maybe there's a loophole for sisters. Maybe you just need to ask. Like restaurant specials. Sometimes they don't give you the discount unless you say something."

The Merc was parked in front of the school. I buckled myself into the passenger seat. Officer Jenkins was nowhere in sight. Casey handed me the Manny's fajita certificate and peeled out of the driveway.

"Read it," he said.

I quoted: "This certificate entitles the bearer to one complimentary fajita dinner for four. One pound of beef or chicken, flour tortillas, *pico de gallo*, refried beans, rice, and guacamole salad. No substitutions." At the bottom was the long expired expiration date. I frowned at my brother. "So? This is your big clue? This is what your angel powers have gotten you? What do we learn from this? I'll tell you. Nothing."

"Not that part, Jenna. The logo. At the top. The Manny's logo."

I looked at the logo: a series of Mexican sombreros. Underneath was Manny's Tex Mex slogan: *A taste of old Mexico, Texas style.* I snorted a laugh. If Dad had left me with one thing, it was the knowledge that while tasty, Tex-Mex cuisine was not authentic Mexican food.

"Read it, Jenna."

"I just did."

"Read it again. Out loud."

"You read it, if it's so thrilling to you. Have you been smoking again?"

"Jesus, Jenna."

"You really shouldn't take the Lord's name in vain, you know. That AIC must mark your demerit sheet every five seconds."

He rolled his eyes. "Mexico, Jenna!"

I smirked. I knew I was annoying him. But not half as much as he was annoying me. *Quid pro quo*, if he still insisted on keeping secrets from me, even now.

"What about Mexico?"

"Mom keeps insisting that Dad's gone to Mexico."

That got me quiet. But it still didn't add up to anything.

"Didn't you ever wonder about Dad's note and this gift

coupon, Jenna? I did. Not right away—everything was such a crazy mess. But later, I thought about it. He leaves this short note. *Y'all take care. I love you.* We all know it by heart. We read the damn thing a million times. But the coupon. I never could figure that out. Did he just set the certificate there by mistake? Or maybe he wanted us to have one last good meal. After awhile, I stopped thinking about it. I had to. Only today I started wondering."

I knew exactly what he meant. I had tried to block that day out of my head, too. The day our dad left us: April 22, five years plus eight months ago. The day everything changed. Whatever had happened to the Samuels family since then all tied back to that one April 22.

"Jenna," Casey said softly, his hands gripping the steering wheel and his eyes focused on the street. "What if it wasn't random that Dad left us that Manny's certificate? I know Mom's not all there right now, but what if on this one thing, she really is? I think this is our clue. I think Dad meant for us to find it."

My heart bounced a couple extra times. I refused to get my hopes up again (damn you, Mags!), even if I agreed that Dad probably wasn't dead. No offense to Mom or anything, but her mumbling that Dad's disappearance had something to do with Mexico—a word on the Manny's gift certificate— was about as thin a connection as anyone could come up with.

I sighed. "Let's say you're right. Let's say that for some reason this was our clue. It's been so long, Casey. What good is it going to do us?"

We were passing a CVS Pharmacy. The Merc shuddered as Casey yanked the wheel. He pulled into the lot and shoved the gear shift into Park.

"I have to try, Jenna." The pained, determined look on my brother's face made him look a whole lot older and smarter than usual. And it wasn't just because he was more handsome now, either. "If I don't try, then what was the whole point?"

He looked away, and then looked back. "And yeah, you were right. Half a joint only, though. Okay? Way early this morning after I dropped you off. So don't worry about me driving. You shoulda heard my cell phone go off. Sounded like a fire engine in my pocket. Scared me half to death, if I wasn't already dead. Ha! Jesus."

He ran a perfectly steady hand through his perfect hair, a gesture that might have appeared anxious on a shaky and disheveled living person. But it didn't, which made *me* anxious. It looked like a high-budget but poorly-acted movie clip of anxiety. For the first time ever, the last thing I was disturbed about was Casey driving stoned.

"Amber was pissed, let me tell you," he said. "Supremely hacked off. For a couple of minutes, she made it seem like they were gonna revoke the whole thing. Maybe even send me to the other place. Although if that's what sends you to the other place, it must be pretty damn crowded."

I bit my lip, hard. I wondered if there was ever going to be a point where my mouth didn't want to drop open every time my brother said something. Casey had never been one to spill out his feelings like monkeys tipping from the barrel. Now he was telling me stuff, or what he could. But I got something now: I couldn't blame him for keeping secrets. It was Amber's fault. She was his one connection to whatever came "after," and she was holding back on *him*. That stupid lump returned to my throat. All the gut-sharing came with A-word territory. He was awkward at it because he was still Casey. That hadn't changed. Or possibly he just didn't want me to realize he didn't know what the hell he was doing.

"Amber's meeting us at home," he went on while I tried to process. "Mom's blood work came back. There's something fishy there, too. But what we need to do is try to remember every single thing that happened that day in April."

I shrugged and nodded.

"I also called Bryce. I looked up Manny's online and they've got this whole room with vintage pinball machines and video games. You know how Bryce loves all that shit. So I asked him what he knew about Manny's Real Tex Mex. Turns out he knows a guy who's hung out there since they opened. When I told him the whole story—well not the whole story—but when I told him about Dad, the guy Bryce knows says he *remembers* Dad. Bryce showed him the author photo from *60 Different Sauces*. And another picture I let him borrow. So we've got someone to talk to at least."

I blinked. "Do you honestly believe that some geek friend of Bryce's is gonna remember Dad being there five years ago?"

Casey gave me the familiar (when alive and stoned) stop-asking-questions-like-an-idiot glare. "You have a better idea?"

I shook my head.

So there we were—sitting in the CVS parking lot in Mamaw Nell's borrowed Mercury Marquis, our only real clues to Dad's disappearance an expired fajita dinner gift certificate from Manny's Real Tex Mex, diluted snake poison in my boots and whatever was now running around in Mom's bloodstream. Basically, a whole lot of weirdness that added up to precisely squat.

But I wasn't in detention. I'd finished my Algebra homework in class, and my persuasive essay wasn't due until next

week. My brother the guardian A-word was more motivated than . . . well, he'd ever been motivated. Take that, Asshat Collins!

Plus, if things started going south, Amber—guardian A-word of my guardian A-word—seemed to have our backs. What else did we need?

Probably a whole lot. Because there was always "chaos theory," after all. Amber had given herself an out. What a convenient excuse for things going south. The "seemed" in "seemed to have our backs" once again "seemed" a lot more like prettying up something that was Bryce-ugly.

Jenna's Journal

December 8th
LATER

Jenna's New Philosophy of Life
Old Jenna: Go along. Live your life. Shit happens. Do the best you can.

New Jenna: Realize that you probably haven't been paying attention AT ALL to the things you should have been noticing. Whatever you *think* just happened, you better trade in for a better thinking cap. Do you really think you understand a plain old car accident? It's just the tip of the iceberg. You haven't been paying attention, remember? You better catch up quick or you're going to be very sorry. Maybe it's already too late.

Note to self: Find out why most philosophies—except maybe for that of crazy cult leaders who get whatever they want because they've brainwashed folks—are extremely depressing. Mags would know.

"WHOSE CAR IS that?" I asked as we rumbled up the driveway. There was an Audi sedan parked in front of our house.

Whoever was driving had no doubt heard our arrival. The Merc needed a new muffler. Possibly an entire exhaust system. I hoped Mamaw Nell wasn't going to blame it on us. She didn't seem the type, but you never knew. Maybe she would wake up one morning and realize that she'd loaned her car to a guardian A-word who was still trying to kick his marijuana habit. Casey better eat those snickerdoodles before she caught on to his angel chicanery.

"Never seen it before," Casey said.

We climbed out of the Merc. Both of us gawked at the Audi. Shiny black exterior, tan leather interior. No *Soylent Green is People* bumper sticker, like the Merc. Dave's idea, but Mamaw Nell thought it was funny.

Soylent Green was this Sci-Fi movie from the 70s. (Dave was a jerk, but he did have decent taste in quirky movies.) The plot: In the future, old folks like Mamaw Nell just disappear. Eventually the main character discovers that they're being killed and turned into organic food pellets. So he runs around like an idiot shouting the quote on the bumper sticker. I guess the idea of people eating ground up oldsters tickled Mamaw Nell's fancy.

"Do you think Amber got rid of the Camaro?" My wiggly stomach knot had returned, and I wasn't exactly sure why. It's not like I had a phobia of expensive automobiles. But unless Amber had traded up, we had a mystery visitor on our hands.

Casey didn't answer. He didn't have to. Amber screeched down the street and motored up behind the Audi.

"Casey Samuels," she barked, swinging out of the Camaro and pounding up the driveway. "You pull any more stunts like that and you are out."

Casey turned noticeably pale. For a second, he almost

looked the way he did before the accident. "It was just half a joint," he said sheepishly. "I barely inhaled."

"Who are you, Bill Clinton? It's not just the pot. It's the secret phone calls to your ex. I vouched for your character. I've never done that before." She paused. "If you want to piss off the AIC, you might want to think about what could happen. Let's just say a certain guy hasn't been real happy since the AIC got pissed at *him*. Oh, he talks a good game—all that 'better to reign in you-know-where than serve in Heaven . . .'"

All at once, she ran out of steam. Her shoulders slumped. She closed her eyes.

Casey and I glanced at each other.

"What is it?" I asked. "What are you trying to tell us?"

"It's all a lie," she said.

I swallowed. My heart kicked into overdrive again.

"*What* is?" Casey spat.

"There is no AIC," she admitted. Her eyes remained hidden under her bangs. "It's just me. Stuck here in Houston until I get Casey to do the right thing. I thought it would be easier if I let you think there was a whole committee. But that's not how it works. Well not exactly. Shit," she said again. "I—you're my first angel to supervise. I'm flying blind here. So to speak."

Casey let out a bitter bark of a laugh. "You lied to me?" he snapped, three times in a row. He slapped his hands against his chest for emphasis of different words, like he was doing a Robert De Niro impression. (You *lied* to me? *You* lied to me? You lied to *me*?)

"Yes. I lied." Amber took a deep breath, regaining her composure, and looked up. Her blue eyes glowed and flickered. "Now I told you the truth. We really don't need to discuss it further. We have questions to answer." She sounded like a typical grown-up asshat, like Mr. Collins, telling me that I still had detention without bothering to explain why. She jerked her head at the Audi. "Whose car is that?"

Casey sneered. He was too miffed to speak. I couldn't blame him.

"We don't know," I muttered. "Listen, Amber, I'm madder than my brother right now, if you can believe it. I don't trust you. You know that. Enough with the lies and the secrets and the BS. Tell us both something that you haven't told either of us yet."

Her jaw tightened. "Fair enough. For one: There really are rules. They just don't kick in until you're acclimated, which for you is taking awhile. And don't get all beside yourself again, Casey. You know it's true. So here's the deal: You can guard Jenna. You're more or less invulnerable. You can sense stuff. But your wings? Those are a one-time deal. You spread them all the way and fly? Well that's it. You're done. You've used your option, and you leave this world forever—" She broke off, as if she was going to add one more thought.

Casey and I glanced at each other again. Neither of us spoke. What the hell could we have possibly said to *that*? I will say this, though: For the first time since I'd gotten to know Amber Velasco, I had almost no doubt she was telling the truth. She looked as if she were about to cry, in fact.

"Can we go inside now?" she demanded.

With a small nod, Casey fumbled for his keys and opened the door. He yanked the worn Manny's gift certificate out of his back pocket. "We're gonna talk about this, though."

Mom was sitting on the couch in the living room. She actually looked halfway presentable. She'd put on clean sweats and one of my old Razorbacks T-shirts. Dr. Chest Hair Renfroe sat next to her. His gaze swung from me to

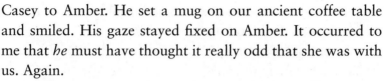

Casey to Amber. He set a mug on our ancient coffee table and smiled. His gaze stayed fixed on Amber. It occurred to me that *he* must have thought it really odd that she was with us. Again.

"Friend of the family now," she said lightly. "These Samuels folks just can't stop showing their gratitude."

Casey laughed nervously. So did I.

Renfroe nodded, his smile wavering. He didn't look convinced. I didn't blame him. All at once, I panicked. Was there more wrong with me? Had he come to tell us that the Cipro wasn't really going to do enough? That he'd found something wacky mixed with the snake venom and that was why I still felt a mite pukey? Or worse, that the blood Amber had surreptitiously drawn had come back from the lab and that *Mom* was dying? Maybe that's why Amber had come screeching up in the first place! Besides, Renfroe might have no idea about Amber's little move. He wasn't her "friend at the lab." Maybe he and Mom were sitting there reviewing my funeral plans. Then why did she look so happy?

"Y'all are home early," she remarked breezily. "Look who's here." She turned to the doc. "Stuart, you have been such an angel to me, visiting all the time."

Casey stiffened.

Be careful how you toss that A-word around, Mom.

Right. Dr. Renfroe had to leave. Now. As much as I appreciated his genius and kindness with the vitamins for Mom and all, this was not the time. And it wasn't like we could just announce: "Hey. There's something nasty going on in Mom's bloodstream and it may be connected to Dad's disappearance and the reason I was going downhill faster than a toddler on a runaway tricycle. You need to leave now so Amber the EMT angel can explain what the tests showed. Which, even if she wasn't a supernatural being, would still be off the record since she took the blood on her own time."

"Sweet ride out there," my brother said to Dr. Renfroe. "That Audi belong to you?"

The doc nodded. "Had it a couple weeks now. But I kept my truck. That way I can still haul stuff." He looked ill at ease. Maybe he felt bad showing off the wealth around us. After all, he would have fired Mom if she hadn't quit first. He stood and turned to me. "How are you feeling, Jenna?"

"Fine," I said.

"You look good. Here. Stick out your tongue." He checked over my throat and my eyes, nodding as he poked and prodded. "How are your feet?"

I shrugged. "I miss my boots. But they feel better."

"Did you change shifts?" Amber asked the doc. "I thought you worked the ER tonight."

"Who are you again?" Mom asked, staring at Amber blankly.

"Amber, Mom—remember?" Casey said. "She's the paramedic who took care of Jenna after our car accident."

"What? Accident?" Mom's hand fluttered to her mouth. I could see the veins pulsing blue under her skin. "I—I do remember now. Why did I forget? I've been forgetting a lot of things these days, haven't I?" Her eyes started to water, of course, like they always did when she forgot something vitally important, such as to take care of her children. "I think maybe I need to lie down now."

In an instant, she slumped, boneless-seeming, against the couch pillows. She looked less like a human and more like a jellyfish. Again, for the zillionth time, I willed myself not to cry, too. Casey stepped around the coffee table and sat himself on the other side of Mom. He was still clutching the

Manny's gift certificate, but set it on the coffee table next to Renfroe's keys. Then he took both of Mom's hands in his.

"It'll be okay," he said.

Dr. Renfroe nodded, still seeming troubled. "You rest now, Holly," he said. "I need to be going now anyway. I'll be back in a couple of weeks." He turned to me. "And of course I'll keep an eye on Jenna here." He bent to grab the keys on the coffee table, pausing over the expired Manny's certificate. I felt my face flush. My neck, too. What if Renfroe thought we were so poor and desperate that we were trying to use expired certificates to get cheap food?

"Cleaning up around here," I said. "We need to throw that away. You ever been there, Doc? Manny serves up some pretty good enchiladas."

Dr. Renfroe tried to smile. He looked almost as queasy as I felt. Maybe he preferred tamales.

"Stuart," my mother said in a quavering voice. She tightened her grasp on my brother's hands. "Mike might be in Mexico. Did you know that?"

"What?" He swallowed audibly. I wondered how crazy he thought Mom was. Jabbering about the husband who abandoned her five years after the fact, apropos of nothing. Of course, if I told him the rest of it, he'd drag us all to the loony bin.

Mom started crying. A little bit of color returned to Dr. Renfroe's cheeks. Now it just looked like he felt sorry for her again. Poor guy. It had to be especially tough for him to see her like this. When she worked for him at Oak View, Mom had been the speech therapist for the neurological cases: folks with Alzheimer's and people recovering from meningitis or encephalitis or anything that might have screwed with their short- or long-term memories. She taught them how to talk again, how to swallow. Dad always used to say he never understood how it didn't just depress the hell out of her to work with people who couldn't remember who they were some days. But it never did.

And then she became one.

(Incidentally, "irony" was never nearly as favorite a vocabulary word as "flummox" or "chicanery.")

Dr. Renfroe moved to the door. "Jenna, I want to see you again next week. Call Houston Northside and ask for my office there. The nurse will set you up with an appointment. No need for the ER again unless you take a turn for the worse."

I wasn't fond of how that sounded, but I guess that's how doctors talked.

"Amber can watch out for you, too, I suppose," he added slowly. He seemed to be her sizing up again, almost as if he didn't recognize her. Well, why would he? She was a random EMT chick. Did he sense something about her now? Like, that she was a total imposter? This whole angel thing was making me a jittery mess. I'd always been good at keeping secrets, but we'd moved to a whole different level. I was beginning to wonder about Maggie's philosophy. Maybe the universe should have just let a pigeon crap on my head.

"I'll keep an eye on them," Amber said. "Thanks, Doctor."

He nodded. "Y'all take care now."

I let out a huge sigh of relief when Casey finally closed the front door behind him.

Mom flashed a weak smile. "Stuart says I can come back to work when I'm feeling better. I keep trying to make myself go, you know. But then the day goes by and here I am."

Amber flashed a grin: odd, considering the circumstances.

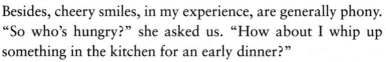

Besides, cheery smiles, in my experience, are generally phony. "So who's hungry?" she asked us. "How about I whip up something in the kitchen for an early dinner?"

I hoped this was code for: *Let's go to the kitchen so I can tell you about the blood work and not freak out your mother.* If it wasn't, and she actually thought offering her personal chef skills was the best use of her angel powers, she and I would need to talk.

Casey helped Mom to her bedroom.

I trailed behind Amber. Just for show—I hoped—she peered into our fridge. It was pretty bleak in there. I tried to assess the look on her face. The last thing I needed right now was my brother's angel boss feeling sorry for us. I may have trusted Amber Velasco a little more than I had before, but I still didn't want her nosing around. In case she was wondering, our freezer contained a half empty ice-cube tray, two hot dogs with freezer burn, the remaining frozen Canadian bacon pizza from the stash Casey had bought when Kroger put them on sale for 50 cents each, and a bag of frozen blueberries that had seen better days.

I cut to the chase. "You really planning on cooking us a meal?"

"You hungry?"

Casey reappeared. Amber slammed the fridge shut and straightened.

"Your mother's got some kind of strange drug in her system," she said without any preliminaries. "Terry at the lab hasn't been able to fully identify it. Just like no one's figured out yet what substance was mixed with the snake venom in your poisoned boots. Truth? Terry and I think we're dealing with the same source even if the two drugs are different." She paused, staring at me with what almost looked like concern.

"Go on," Casey demanded.

"Whatever was in your system, Jenna, was meant to make you sick or kill you. But the drug we've identified in your mom isn't nearly as lethal. It's more psychotropic, but not exactly. So far, all Terry's been able to isolate is that it has some herbal properties, like the ginkgo biloba you buy over the counter to boost memory. But like I say, that's not it. He says he needs another day or so."

Neither Casey nor I responded. My legs felt wobbly. Amber would have made a good doctor. She spoke about horrible shit with total clinical detachment.

"Trust me, this guy's a genius," she added. "He'll figure it out."

Or maybe not. Now she sounded like an idiot. "Is he an angel, too?" I asked.

"Nope. Not yet, anyway." A wistful grin flitted across her lips. Okay, creepy. Did she want this guy to die so they could be angel boyfriend and girlfriend? Better to let that sleeping dog lie. Who the hell knew what Amber really wanted? That was still a big question smack in the middle of this mess.

Casey scowled. "What do we do? How's it getting into her system? Should we check her shoes? Her clothes? Her sheets? It's not like she goes a lot of places. Damn it, Amber. I figured someone was getting at Jenna's boots at school, like when she was in PE or something. But Mom hasn't left our property for a year except the other night to the hospital. Are you saying that she and my sister were—are—being drugged right here in this house?"

I swallowed. My brother might be failing classes, but he wasn't stupid and I didn't think it was the marijuana, either. The look on his face said it all: He wanted to keep us safe, and he was failing at it. I thought back to those first weeks

when Dad had disappeared. I'd walked into Casey's room one night and found him kneeling at his bed, his elbows resting on the mattress, hands clasped together. "Please let me find him," he'd repeated over and over as I stood silent in the doorway. "Please. I'll do anything you ask. Please." It was the last time I'd heard my brother pray.

"We need to check everything that your mother eats and drinks," Amber said. "Especially anything that you two don't. That'll be a start."

"Should we have told Renfroe?" Casey asked. "I mean he's looking into Jenna's boot poison and all. Maybe he—"

"No." Amber's tone was sharp.

Casey's brows scrunched. "Why not?"

"Because I'm dealing with your mother's situation, not him. Doctor-patient confidentially."

"You're not even a doctor!" I practically shouted.

My brother's gaze met mine. Here's what I understood right then: Casey wasn't really sure about anything when it came to being an A-word. But he was going to find out what happened to Dad. He was going to uncover what had been destroying our family and why. He wasn't going to stop until he did. Hell, maybe Lanie Phelps had glimpsed that same spark of motivation inside him, something she hadn't seen since he was a football player. It went a long way to making a crap situation less crappy.

"So what do you want to do now, Casey?" Amber asked, sounding defeated.

"I want to go to Manny's. Bryce says there's someone I need to talk to."

"And you believe him," Amber said. It wasn't a question. It was an accusation.

Casey pulled out his cell phone and dialed.

I decided to use the painfully awkward silence to take inventory of our fridge, to see if there was anything Mom and I ate that could be destroying her brain and turning my pee green at the same time. (Amber *had* said the poisons came from the same source.) The list of items Mom consumed that weren't leftovers brought home by Casey had extended to five: toast, water, juice, bananas, hard boiled eggs.

Casey was deep in conversation with Bryce. "You sure?" he kept repeating. He nodded. Drummed his fingers on our grimy kitchen counter. "Okay. If you're screwing with me, I quit." He shoved his phone back in his pocket and glanced at Amber. "Bryce says we're good to go. Dude's name is Zeke. Bryce showed him an old sports column of Dad's—you know, the ones where he had a byline and his picture. Zeke swears he remembers seeing Dad at Manny's—probably more than once. Bryce is smart like that."

This was the first I'd heard of Bryce's IQ. My personal experience had been that a guy who alphabetized his comic book collection by size and thickness was not exactly using his God-given brains to their fullest extent. On the other hand, my brother the angel was still failing Teen Leadership. The world was a funny place.

"And?" Amber waved her hand in a rolling circle, the universal sign for get to the point.

"And he'll be there until Manny's closes around ten. I'm going to go see him. Talk to him in person. It's a start. You and Jenna need to stay here with Mom. I'll call if I find out anything."

"No way," Amber and I said in unison.

"But—"

"Casey!" A muscle tightened in Amber's shapely jaw. "No buts. You're new. *You do what I tell you.*"

With that, she blew out a breath. Correction: she blew wind into our kitchen. Hurricane force. Just for an instant. The ceiling fan in the breakfast room shook. The light over the sink exploded. The overhead light flickered. The hands on our oven clock—the one that had no battery and had been stuck at 2:21 for the past three years—spun to 2:22, then promptly died again.

"Holy crap," I muttered.

Amber's posture straightened. She seemed to grow taller. A golden glow surrounded her, so bright, that it hurt my eyes. "I'm going with you."

Both Casey and I took a step back.

"Did something fall?" Mom called from the bedroom.

"Light burned out," Casey yelled back. His voice trembled. "Made-in-China bulbs."

"I'm going, too." I set my hands on my hips. If I had my boots, I'd have stomped them on the floor. Amber may have been able to flummox my brother with her angel chicanery, but she could not scare me. Besides, I actually agreed with her on this one. No way would I allow myself to be stuck with her and Mom. "Let's face it. Mom can't get much worse. And someone needs to keep the two of you from killing yourselves."

"Already dead," Amber said. But she smiled.

I didn't smile back. "You're also covered in dust," I said. During her hissy fit, the gobs of dust on the ceiling fan had catapulted into the air and splattered her EMT shirt.

"I'll loan you something," I told her helpfully.

She gave me the stink eye. Whatever. I'd have done the same.

We left the house about twenty minutes later. Amber was wearing her EMT pants and my old pink T-shirt that read,

"This Ain't My First Rodeo." I was still in my jeans, tank and hoodie. While I was getting her the shirt, Amber had managed to combine our last banana with the frozen blueberries and the ice cubes into a thin looking smoothie. I made my mother drink it, and when she leaned back on her pillows and her eyes fluttered shut, Casey kissed her on the cheek.

"You sleep."

It was almost dark outside, and the Gilroy's had plugged in their decorations. The two yard angels glowed like spaceships in the middle of their lawn. On our driveway, my two angels narrowed their eyes at each other.

"What's the matter now?" Amber muttered. "Are you too stoned to drive?"

"That's what I'm talking about," he said evenly. "You may be my boss, but you need to lose the damn attitude."

"Whatever. You can drive. But the car better not smell like marijuana."

"It's Mamaw Nell's," I piped up. "She smokes Pall Malls."

We climbed into the Merc. None of us spoke, but Casey kept stealing angry glances at Amber as he drove. It was the same look he used to give me when we were little and I insisted that he watch *Dora the Explorer* instead of *ESPN*. I watched them nervously from the backseat. Finally, apropos of nothing, he snapped: "It's *my* dad and *my* mom and *my* sister and *my* life. At least it was. I mean isn't that the whole point of you being here? Making sure I do the right thing? So how can I do the right thing, if you keep doing it for me?"

She sighed. "You're right. I can't. However your dad fits into this whole puzzle, I don't know. You two are on your own."

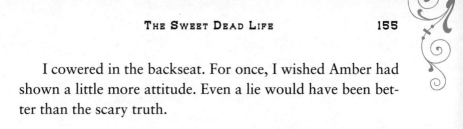

I cowered in the backseat. For once, I wished Amber had shown a little more attitude. Even a lie would have been better than the scary truth.

W hat Casey and I Remembered About the Day our
Father Disappeared:

• The weather was humid but not hot yet. I knew this because
I remembered what I was wearing: the lightweight navy fleece
that said Monterey Aquarium, a souvenir from our trip to
California the previous summer.

• Mom had been late from work. A patient had gone
wandering from the Alzheimer's unit and Oak View went on
lockdown until they found him. Somehow, he made it back
to his room on his own. She came home about nine o'clock.
Back then this was my bed time and I'd just put on my PJs.
The three of us asked each other where Dad was.

• Technically I don't remember this part, but Dad had been to
Manny's Real Tex Mex that day. The gift certificate was our
proof of that, and the confirmation by Bryce's buddy, Zeke.

• Another related memory: I had been to Manny's with Dad. He made a big deal about their chili gravy and how when they got their liquor license, they were going to have ten different Mexican beers on tap. He scribbled it all down in a new spiral notebook. And that disappeared with him. All the old notebooks—packed full of reviews and interviews and descriptions—were still tucked on a shelf in his closet just like always. Now I wondered. Why hadn't Dad told me he was going back?

• Back to the day he went AWOL: When he left the house that morning, he was wearing brown khaki Dockers slacks, topsiders, and a white roll-up-sleeve dress shirt. He climbed into his blue Ford Focus. Mom gave the police the exact same details, and more. He hadn't washed his hair. He'd fiddled with his messenger bag. He'd kissed us and told us that he hadn't slept well. Back then Mom's memory was precise like that. It should have been. She spent all day working to spruce up other people's brains. Like I said: irony. She once knew every memory trick in the book.

• The police had been convinced that Dad had run off. "Was there another woman?" they asked Mom like a zillion times.

ABOUT SIX MONTHS in, Mom decided to believe them. Secretly, I'd given up in a much shorter period of time. Now this made me feel small and guilty. Dad's cell phone had gone right to voicemail every time we called it. Mom had continued to pay for the phone for three years. "She calls his phone to listen to his voice on the message," Casey told me. Eventually he and I admitted to each other that we'd been doing the same thing. But the weirdest part: Someone had started

putting money in Mom and Dad's bank account not long after he disappeared. At first Mom didn't even notice—things were crazy and Dad had always taken care of the finances.

But then the deposits stopped. Just like that.

WE DROVE SOUTH on I-45 into Houston. The air was balmy again. Christmas in Houston was always a crapshoot. Two years ago it had snowed—enough flakes to make an actual snowball. Last year, we walked around in shorts. Right now it was somewhere in between. But everything was twinkling and glowing like the holidays. Manny's Real Tex Mex sat on Westheimer, a little ways off Montrose. The building had been a movie theater back in the day, and the specials were up on the old theater marquee in red block letters. The combo plate looked promising: two cheese enchiladas with chili gravy, two tamales, rice, beans, chips and a bonus taquito with queso.

Tiny beer-bottle-shaped lights hung from strings on the ceiling. Half of the tables were packed with people scarfing down tortilla chips, chugging beer and margaritas. Bruce Springsteen's "Santa Claus is Coming to Town" blared from the loudspeakers.

A smiling, inflatable snowman in a Santa hat and poncho sat in the corner. When we walked by him, his eyes darted back and forth and then he said "*Feliz Navidad*, y'all."

Dad would have loved it. The knot in my stomach returned.

Casey, Amber, and I trooped upstairs. The game room had once been an upstairs lobby for the balcony level. The red-flowered carpet looked worn enough to be the original. It smelled like old carpet, anyway, and the room was stuffed with dozens of flickering screens and ancient pinball machines.

There was only one guy up there, hunched over *Terminator 2*. He thumped the pinging and flapping pinball machine with his hip. "Yeah!" he shouted. He was thin and balding, his twig-like arms hanging out of a T-shirt that read "One taco short of a combo platter." If you added some hair, he could have been Casey's age.

"That must be Zeke," Casey said, confirming our collective worst fears.

Right. So like Bryce, he was probably closer to thirty. On the other hand, it seemed Zeke was a man of intense concentration. At least when it came to pinball. I only hoped it also came to random nights five years and eight months ago. When he didn't look up—even after Casey's third "Hey dude!"—Amber stepped forward.

Suddenly, the lights on the pinball machine blinked out. The little silver ball rolled down the hole and the whole thing went dark.

I frowned at Amber. "I thought you had earthbound limitations," I whispered.

She flicked a finger toward the floor. "Cord's loose," she said.

I followed her gaze to the black extension cord hanging almost out of the wall socket. Zeke jolted and turned around. He looked at the three of us like we'd fallen from the sky. Not far from the truth.

"Bryce told us to see you," Casey said. He sounded like he'd wandered into some old spy movie. *Bryce told us to see you. Do you have the goods?*

Zeke looked disoriented. His beady eyes twitched like he was still watching silver pinballs. "I'm hungry," he said. "Let's grab some grub. I'll tell you what I know."

Zeke, it seemed, was in the same spy movie with Casey.

Amber sighed. "Geeks," she muttered. "Like there weren't enough of them when I was pre-med. I'm cursed. That has to be it."

ZEKE ORDERED THE combo special. Casey and I stuck to ice tea, spending the little money Casey had in his wallet. Amber sipped from her water glass and shot occasional longing glances at the margaritas being slugged down by the ladies at the next table.

I'd have indulged in some taquitos if we had cash. I should have answered Amber honestly back at the house. I *was* hungry.

The waiter—a meaty, muscular guy with very hairy arms and no name tag—eyeballed us as he delivered our table's one and only meal order. The look in his eyes was hard to read, but I think it was saying, *Why are you four cheap losers hogging a table and not ordering food? You definitely don't look like big tippers.*

"Can I get you anything else?" he asked dully.

We shook our heads.

He stomped off, hairy arms swinging at his sides.

I stuffed a couple chips in my mouth and tried not to drool while Zeke forked into the tamale. Mid-chew, he reached into his pocket and dug out a piece of paper. With the drama that matched his weird silence, he unfolded it.

My father's byline photo stared up at us.

My mouthful of chips stuck in my throat. Casey was right. And screw it: Zeke deserved to be as geeky and dramatic and spy-movie-ish as he wanted. Sort of.

"This is the guy," Zeke said around his mouthful of tamale and gravy. He tapped my father's face, leaving a greasy dot of red in the middle of his forehead. "Bryce told you, right? About me?"

Amber smiled without any humor. "About you?"

"Yeah, that I've got one of those memories? If it's connected to a place I ate or a place that supports gamers, then I don't forget." He tapped the same gravy-grease finger to his own forehead. "You can trust me on that."

Casey glared at him. "And?"

Zeke tucked back into his combo plate. He looked a little like that actor Michael Cera. Only if Zeke had been in the Scott Pilgrim movie, he wouldn't have had seven girlfriends, evil or otherwise.

Amber leaned across the Formica table. "Zeke," she said. "I'm not a patient girl. If you have something to tell us, I would suggest you begin talking."

"She's not joking, man," my brother added. "*You* can trust *me* on that."

Zeke nodded. Chewed. Slurped some water through his straw. Our surly waiter appeared. He refilled our chip basket. I waited until he was gone to spot check for stray arm hairs. But before Zeke could dish, Manny himself walked by and waved hello.

I recognized Manny—whom I'd never actually met when I was here with dad—from the picture on the front of the menu. He was in his late forties, really tall—about six foot five I estimated—thin and bald, the shave-your-head kind, not the follicle-challenged kind. Zeke got hyped at Manny's brief appearance. Now that Manny had franchised into Austin and Dallas and San Antonio, Zeke told us, he didn't come around as much. It was like a celebrity sighting or seeing the Pope. At least to Zeke, who chewed some more, then—when we were all on the verge of exploding—finally spat it out.

He was positive that he had seen Dad talking to Manny. On that fateful April 22.

The reason? Or reasons?

Back then Zeke thought he might want a culinary career. He'd taken a couple of cooking classes at Houston Community College and he wasn't half bad as a sous chef. *(Note: I have no idea if the chef part is true. But it's what Zeke said. He was irritating as hell, but I didn't take him for a liar.)* He'd come to the restaurant that day to chat up Manny about a job in the kitchen. Manny had been buying old pinball machines from Bryce, so Zeke figured he had an in.

"I drank like a gallon of iced tea while I was waiting," Zeke told us, finally taking a break from eating. "Your dad and Manny talked a long time. I didn't want to be in the john when Manny got freed up, but the waitress kept bringing out plate after plate of food, and Manny—he was pointing and talking and your dad was tasting and chewing."

"Food writer," I told Zeke. "He was gonna write a book about Tex-Mex."

If this interested Zeke it was hard to tell. He didn't seem to care so much about what had happened to Dad as he did about impressing us with his phenomenal powers of memory. I concentrated on the tortilla chips to keep myself from saying what I wanted to say: *I just hope all these stories are real and not some fancy game-boy chicanery. If they are, I will procure new boots so I can kick your skinny rear end.*

"Anyway," Zeke went on, "I had to piss like a racehorse. Finally, I said the hell with it. But I figured I'd give Manny a heads up before I headed to the john. And that's when it happened."

My ears perked up. I scooted closer.

"I got to their table just as Carla was bringing out combo number 10. That's the one with three different plates, you know? There's a starter plate with a ground beef taco and a chili con queso puff. Then the hot plate: enchiladas and gravy and two tacos al carbon. And then the flan and sopapilla duo for dessert—"

"We don't need the menu details," Amber stated.

Zeke smiled at her. Then he did a double-take, clearly noticing for the first time how attractive she was. "Sorry. I mean normally, they don't bring all that stuff out at once, it's a dining progression. But there was Carla, the whole shebang balanced on her arm. I just brushed against her, I swear. That's when the enchilada plate tipped. Your dad got sauced."

Casey frowned. "He was drunk?"

"No." Zeke pointed to his own combo plate. "Sauced." He tapped a finger to the red chili gravy. "She spilled enchilada gravy on his shirt. Serious spillage. He had a mess of red all down the front."

I glanced at Amber. She rolled her eyes. The rest of Zeke's story went like this: Both Carla and Manny started apologizing. The man Zeke believed to be our father blotted at his shirt with a napkin and then headed to the bathroom. Zeke decided he could hold it until Dad returned. (Manny's bathrooms are one-holers. You're either in or you're out.) Zeke grabbed Manny and chatted him up about the sous chef possibility. Manny gave him a job the next week, and Zeke lasted precisely one shift. Cut himself while chopping onions and bled all over the avocadoes during the dinner rush. When the head cook stopped screaming in Spanish, Zeke realized he'd been fired.

"But here's the weird part," Zeke finished. "Your dad never came back. I knocked on the door and the john was empty. Manny said he was probably steamed about his shirt or had to go back to work. I'd have never thought about it again until Bryce asked me. And then I was like, sure I remember

the guy. He was the one who never came back from the toilet." Zeke scooped a handful of chips and arranged them in the remaining puddle of chili gravy on his plate. "There's a back door. Leads to the rear parking lot."

Amber pressed her lips together. I could see the wheels turning in her head. "What about your father's car?"

"Disappeared with him," Casey said. "It was a blue Ford Focus. Never turned up anywhere. That's what we kept hoping at first, that someone would find his car. Or that he'd use his credit cards or ATM card and there'd be a record. He never did. But there was no sign of foul play, and he'd left us a note. Eventually the cops decided he just wanted to drop off the grid."

I could tell that we were all thinking the same thing. Whatever happened to Dad had started here at Manny's. Something or someone had stopped him from returning to his table. Had he left us the note before or after? Maybe it didn't even matter.

What mattered: Zeke was probably the last person who had seen him. But where had Dad gone after that?

We convinced Zeke to leave his last enchilada and accompany us to the back door, to investigate possible escape routes. Hairy-Armed Waiter kept his eye on us as we passed by. (Possibly he needed other employment. If one table of mostly non-eaters threw him into such a funk, maybe he wasn't cut out for the Tex-Mex life. *Note to self: Find out if Dr. Chest Hair Renfroe has hairy relatives in the food service industry.*)

Standing outside Manny's, I tried to imagine what had gone on. The john's backdoor looked like a john's backdoor. There was a dumpster. There was no secret passage to some other place other than the parking lot. Had Dad left to get a new shirt? Did someone force him to leave? Why? Mike Samuels was a sports reporter and food writer. If he hadn't run off with someone or just gotten tired of being our dad, then what?

We tromped back into the restaurant. Zeke asked if we were going to pay for his dinner. When Amber gave him the stink eye, he headed upstairs to finish his game.

I started toward the front door.

Casey stopped dead in his tracks, staring across the room like a hound dog who'd sighted a squirrel.

There, at a table across the room, wearing jeans and a red sweater over a white shirt with sleeves rolled up above the wrists—her blonde hair pulled into a high ponytail—sat Lanie Phelps. She was with two other girls that I recognized as Spring Creek cheerleaders, crunching on chips and perusing Manny's menu. The other two had beers in front of them. Lanie was sipping what looked like a Coke. She lifted her eyes.

Like in one of those sappy Hallmark movies, her gaze locked with my brother's. She smiled and waved.

"You better not have planned this," Amber hissed.

Casey shook his head. He couldn't stop smiling back at Lanie.

"We need to go," Amber stated.

Lanie hopped from her chair and dashed over. "Hey Casey—" She paused and flashed Amber an impressed once-over. "Love your shirt!"

"My what?" Amber glanced down at my loaner tee, the pink material shining in the glow of Manny's multi-colored beer bottle lights. She planted her hands on her hips. Only now did she probably realize that the shirt bore a "This Ain't My First Rodeo" logo.

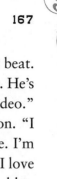

"I'm going in March," Lanie said without missing a beat. "My dad got us front row tickets for most of the shows. He's on the board this year. I just mean that I love the rodeo." She turned to include Casey and me in the conversation. "I do barrel racing. Not at the Houston Rodeo, of course. I'm not that good. Least not yet. But Montgomery County, I love it because . . ." Lanie trailed off. She giggled and covered her mouth, a repeat of what I'd seen before. Only it didn't look like a performance. Her eyes grew serious. But for some reason, they fixed on me. "I'm so sorry. I'm just feeling a little weird. Jenna, your brother told me that you've been sick. I just wanted—"

"I need to talk to you, Lanie," Casey interrupted.

He grabbed up Lanie's hand and led her over by the inflatable snowman with the Santa hat. Lanie hooked her arms around my brother's waist.

"Feliz Navidad, y'all," the inflatable snowman shouted.

Amber made a sound that I can only describe as a growl. She began to stomp after them. Part of me wanted to let her. This was, after all, Lanie Phelps. Instead, I found myself grabbing Amber's arm.

"Let me go, Jenna," she warned.

"Give him a sec," I murmured. "Please."

I had not ever expected to say please to Amber Velasco. Or find myself wanting Casey to get back with the very girl who had dumped him without a second thought. But here I was. Because someday I wanted a boy to look at me like Casey was looking at Lanie. I wanted a boy who would graze his knuckles over my skin and make my breath catch. A nice boy, not a boy like Dave who ogled my boobs every chance he got and never quite looked me in the face.

Amber scowled. She shook free and kept walking. One step. Two. At three, she stopped and turned.

"It can't work out," she said quietly. "You know that, right? Because in case you've forgotten—"

"Shut up," I said. "Please." Did she really think she had to spell it out for me?

Amber's perfect lips twitched. She tugged at her bangs. "It's good that you love him. He needs that, even now. But you have to be realistic, Jenna. Otherwise it's going to hurt even more. For both of you. And for this girl. Trust me. I know."

I raised a finger over my lips, choosing to ignore that last part. Had Amber Velasco loved and lost? Was that part of what she was hiding from us? But it didn't matter. In this moment, right here and now, all I cared about was that she let my brother be. He deserved a split-second of happiness. He deserved a lot more.

Before Amber could consider interfering again, Casey bounded back to us.

"We're going out first Saturday of Christmas vacation," Casey said breathlessly.

Amber and I watched as Lanie returned to the cheer squad, now on their second round of beers. She was the designated driver, Casey added. He'd checked.

"She's changed, Jenna," he whispered.

Amber sighed again, but made no comment. Neither did I. Because really, what could I tell him that he didn't already know deep down? Some things you have to come to on your own. Even Casey knew that.

BACK IN THE Merc on the way home, Casey was chatty and full of energy. Not a big surprise, though it perked up my stomach knot.

"Let's say Mom is right. Dad's contacting her and he's

scared. And let's say I'm right, too. Jenna was poisoned because someone wants him to resurface, because they know he'd do anything to save his daughter. But that someone also doesn't want Mom to interfere. That's why they're giving her the drugs to make her crazy. If Dad does resurface, they want him in the weakest possible condition. They want him totally vulnerable. Amber, you said the drugs were probably from the same source, right?"

"Probably," Amber said in a faraway voice.

I kept quiet. I wondered if she was thinking the same thing. That Casey was "projecting." That his theory was based on something very simple and sad: Casey still wanted Dad to be the kind of guy *he* was. The kind of guy who would do anything to save someone he loved. I leaned back. Then scooted forward again. Something was poking me in the ass. I swiveled and dug my hand cautiously into the funky smelling seat cushions.

Another envelope of pictures. Mamaw Nell sure liked to document her casino trips. At least they were a distraction.

I lay full out on the seat and squinted at the collection. With the Christmas lights threaded on the trees along Westheimer, I was able to see enough.

There was Mamaw Nell and her friends clinking their margarita glasses together. Another one of them in front of the Merc. Mamaw Nell was holding a cigarette between her fingers. The rest of the photos were all taken at the casino. Nell and her friends, putting coins in the slots. Posed in line at the all-you-can-eat seafood buffet pointing at the King Crab legs. Nell at the craps table, standing next to some lady toting an oxygen tank. I had never been, but it looked like the casinos at Lake Charles were like nursing homes with gambling.

I flipped through the rest. They were pretty much the

same. In the last picture, Mamaw Nell was standing by a Double Cherry slot machine, smiling and pointing. Looked like she'd won a jackpot that day. Everyone was looking at her; even the people on the far right walking out of the poker room. Everybody seemed happy for her. Well, almost everybody. One skinny guy in the back, younger and swarthy, was pulling at his hair. His mouth was open in mid-shriek. He was the only one not looking at Mamaw Nell. Instead he was staring at the camera.

My heart started to thump.

This guy wasn't just some random sucker who'd lost everything at a casino. I sat up. Reached for the dusty dome light. My stomach knot wiggled like a fish on a line.

"Holy shit." I said, "Stop the car! Pull over."

As we had recently been in a traumatic vehicular situation, my brother complied without question. He screeched into an angled space at the Valero station on the corner. He said a few words that I won't repeat. Amber said a few, too.

I shoved the picture into the gap between the front seats. "Look! The guy in the back on the right." I leaned over so I could see their reactions.

They looked.

Amber sucked in a breath. "Sonofabitch."

"Sonofabitch," Casey concurred.

"Exactly," I said. "This is the same guy who says he's not a gambler."

We sat in the Valero parking lot staring at the guy in the picture. The one walking out of the poker room at Isle of Capri Casino in Lake Charles, who looked like he'd lost his last dime. The one who was so upset that he couldn't even fake a happy look for Mamaw Nell's nickel-slot jackpot. The one with the familiar tuft of manly chest hair poking out of

his collared shirt. The one who had been in our world a lot lately.

Dr. Stuart Renfroe.

Thank you, Mags, I thought. I'd been looking for the universe to provide a giant pigeon turd, and here it was.

"Amber," I said. "What do you think about coincidences?"

"A lot of them are just that," she said. "Coincidences. But some things definitely happen for a reason."

She held the picture to the light, studying it some more.

"Look at him. That is not a happy camper."

I had not pegged Amber as a woman who used the phrase 'happy camper.' But we had more important things to worry about right now. "The point is, he *lied*," I said. "He said he wasn't a gambler. What the hell is he doing at a casino, then?"

Casey shook his head. "This is bad."

"I am really glad I didn't give him your mother's sample," Amber said, so quietly I could barely hear her.

Here is what we pondered as we sat in the Merc under the harsh glow of the Valero station, staring at a slightly bent photo that had poked me in the ass: Dr. Stuart Renfroe looked like a man in trouble. Maybe he was. Maybe he wasn't. But one thing we knew for sure: he was a liar.

What we were really pondering: Who else would have been able to poison both Mom and me? Aside from Casey, he was the only other human being who had been in our house on a semi-regular basis.

Casey shoved the Merc in gear. "We need to go home," he said. "We need to check on Mom." We tore out of the parking lot, bouncing as we hit the road. The Merc's shocks were non-existent.

"He drops by a lot, right?" Amber asked.

"Since she stopped going to work, definitely," Casey said.

I thought harder. "Before that, too, right, Casey? When she started getting so depressed about Dad being gone. He came by a few times. Brought us pizza once. Some sandwiches."

No. It couldn't be. But maybe it was. The chips I'd eaten began to wrangle in my stomach. Why hadn't I ever thought about it before? On the other hand, why would I? Mom had stopped functioning. People gave us the pity stare every time we used the food stamp card. Dr. Renfroe's contribution had seemed like luck to me. Especially the vitamins—

"Crap," I said out loud. "Stupid idiot."

"What?" Casey kept his gaze on the road, but Amber turned to look at me.

"Those free samples," I said. "It's got to be. Damn it, Casey. Those vitamins I give Mom every day? The ones we can't afford? Care of Dr. Renfroe? It's the only thing she puts in her body that you and I don't."

It was like lifting a curtain, only to realize that what was on the other side was the worst thing you could possibly imagine, too.

"Drive faster," I urged my brother. "Hurry."

Was I really as healthy as I'd felt these past couple of days? If Renfroe wasn't who he claimed to be, and also basically my only doctor, then there were no guarantees. Everything he'd told me replayed in my brain on fast-forward. I could be dying again. Granted, we were all basing this wild hypothesis on a random photo we'd found in the back of Mamaw Nell's Merc. He could have been volunteering at the casino to make sure that none of the old fogeys keeled over and died. But, no: Something about him was off. Somehow,

for whatever reason, we'd been given a glimpse of the *real* Dr. Renfroe. Just like I'd glimpsed his chest hair when I woke up in the ER.

"Be careful," Amber said to Casey.

She didn't tell him to slow down.

We debated how to dispose of the vitamins. First, we tucked some in a baggie so Amber could let her lab friend analyze them. Then we searched the house for vitamin bottles. Mom had one on her nightstand. I found another under her sink where she'd stored all those hair color products. A couple more sat on the top shelf of our mostly empty pantry.

"Flush 'em," my brother said.

"You can't," Amber told him. "You want whatever's in them to filter into the water supply?"

"Does everything you flush filter into the water supply?" Casey asked.

It was a reasonable question, but we had no time. "Just throw them all away," I said. I peeled off the latex gloves I'd worn while we searched. Amber had given us each a pair from her EMT bag just in case. "There's all sorts of stuff in landfills. If we wrap the bottles, it'll be like a century before it seeps out, right?"

Note to self: I needed to work on my ecological con-cerns. Not that I'd ever call Al Gore about the ins-and-outs of letting evil vitamins into the environment. But this was Texas. We used to be our own country. We could handle it.

Talking to Mom would have to wait. She'd slept through our vitamin scavenger hunt, even through a haphazard sort of physical. (Amber had given her a quick once-over—or as best she could without removing the ever-present sweat-pants and T-shirt—making sure Mom's condition hadn't deteriorated while we were gone.) By then it was two in the morning.

"You need to get some sleep," Casey said to me.

Instead, I flopped down on the floor outside Mom's bed-room. Casey sighed and joined me, leaning against the closed door. Amber sat cross-legged next to him.

"Not tired," I said, yawning. My eyes drooped closed.

WHEN I CAME to, Casey was still sitting with his back against Mom's door. He appeared to be sleeping. From what I could see through the family room windows it was still dark outside, but getting lighter. Amber was gone.

I watched my brother sleep. He *did* look different. Not just the stuff I could see on the surface. Even passed out against the door, his expression hinted at something I couldn't quite place. Peace? A little. But there was a hint of something sad, too, which made him seem older. But most of all he looked strong. Especially his hands. They weren't lined or wrinkled or anything, but underneath that new bronzy sheen, they seemed sturdier. Like they could lift you right up.

Casey's eyes snapped open.

I flinched. It was like he'd been watching me with his eyes closed. "Um, morning," I said.

"You need to get ready for school. I'm gonna wake up Mom in a minute. Figure out what to tell her and ask her about Dr. Renfroe."

"You don't sleep anymore, do you?" I asked.

"Not really." He laughed and shook his head. "I can make myself doze off. But it's not the same. It's not, um, involuntary?" His voice rose in a question like even he wasn't quite sure—not that he didn't have to sleep, but how it all worked.

"Did you sit here all night watching me?"

"Well, sort of. And thinking about stuff, you know."

At first I figured he meant Renfroe and all that was going on. But he blushed, just a little, and I guessed at what had really been on his mind.

"Lanie, huh?" It was the first time I'd ever said her name in the past year without wanting to scream or cackle or puke.

The blush deepened. He jumped to his feet, avoiding my eyes in the pre-dawn glow trickling through our filthy windows. "We'll see. It's weird, I know. But I—I liked her so much, Jenna. I really did. I guess I never stopped. And I know you never did, but she's different now. Honestly, when I told her how sick you were—"

"How much *did* you tell her?" I interrupted.

"Nothing specific. Just that you and Mom had been sick. But the thing is, she never asked about either of y'all before. It's not just about me, is what I'm saying. So she wants to go on a date. She wants to make up for things. Does that make any sense?"

I rubbed my eyes. "I don't know," I said after a long minute. "I'm only in the eighth grade."

He laughed. "Good point. I'll keep it PG-13. It's only a date, Jenna. One date."

He was silent then. I waited with him through the quiet.

I was going to leave it at that, actually. But my question bubbled up and out before I could stop it. "If we figure this all out, if we find Dad—will you be just gone?" This was bigger than Lanie Phelps. Bigger than any piece of all the craziness.

Casey looked surprised. Had he not thought about this?

"I don't know," he said. But he didn't sound afraid, just matter-of-fact. "Amber won't tell me. Maybe she doesn't know, either. I'm getting the impression they don't trust her much up there."

So he had asked. It was also good to know that "they" (whoever "they" might be) were suspicious of her, too. Not in the big ways, obviously. But she clearly still had a lot of explaining to do, and not just to us.

"Where *is* she, anyway? Amber the annoying?"

"Ha! Don't call her that to her face. She'll be back. Not sure when. Soon, though."

"Whatever." I was suddenly cranky and my back felt stiff from sleeping on the floor. The nausea that I'd had for so long was mostly gone, but it still lingered in the back of my throat. I hoisted myself up and stretched.

"You're still taking your Cipro, right?" Casey asked. "Maybe you need another IV." He studied me like he could assess this from looking. "Just not from Renfroe."

Without warning, he pulled me into a hug. My face mashed against his shoulder. I blinked, unable to do anything but smell that nice smell of his.

"Did dying hurt?" I asked against his shirt, my heart thumping. "Were you scared?"

Casey was quiet so long I wondered if he'd heard me.

"Yeah," he said. "It did. Yeah, I was. But not for long," he added. "I came back quick, Jenna. I came back for you."

My eyes started leaking as I remembered looking over at Casey in the car.

"I'll stay as long as I can," he whispered. "I promise. I won't leave y'all if I can help it." He let go and ruffled my hair in a big brotherly way that he'd never done before. "Who else could put up with all your crap?"

Before I could think of a suitable insult, he knocked on Mom's door and opened it. She stirred and sat up in bed. She stared at us for a long while.

Then she managed a weak smile. "Since when did you start holding your sister's hand?"

What Casey Told Mom:

Your vitamins have been recalled. Nothing to worry about, just the Number 40 red dye was defective. Best not to take anything for a few days.

If any new bottles appear, don't take any of those, either. The vitamin company has no idea how many batches were messed up. Better safe than sorry.

QUESTIONING HER ABOUT Dr. Chest Hair was trickier. She remembered (mostly) that he had helped me at the hospital. She said—definitely—that he came to visit every couple weeks. That was all we knew for sure. Her memory was like a knotted shoelace that you end up throwing away because you don't have the patience to untangle it.

I thought about how nice Renfroe had been to me, how gentle and concerned.

"When he was here," I asked Mom, "what did y'all talk about?"

Casey sighed. We'd asked Mom this every which way we could think of. She hadn't come up with any answer.

"Work, maybe?" I persisted. "They must really miss you at Oak View."

I figured it was a nice thing to say. I'd never had a job, but Mom had loved hers. It was one of the things that kept her from falling apart in that first year after Dad disappeared. The patients she worked with needed her, just like we did. Dr. Renfroe needed her, for God's sake.

My chest tightened. Had Renfroe been faking how he felt about Mom? How could we have been so wrong? When she first started getting too depressed and nervous to go out, she worried about this sort of thing: how the Doc and all those patients would get by without her.

I watched Mom's face. Maybe it was my imagination, but something flickered there. One thing triggered something else and the wheels started cranking like the swirly dash display in our poor deceased Prius.

"People were dying, you know," my mother said. She winced, as if shocked the words had come out of her mouth.

"What?" Casey asked, now riveted.

Mom's eyes started to glaze over and then snapped back in focus. I turned away, an old habit. It hurt too much. Would she ever get well from whatever was gnawing at her system? I pictured it inside her like one of those disgusting nutria that swam in the pond near our house. Wharf rats, people called them. Big ugly rodents the size of beavers, chewing on Mom's brain. I'd only been sick for a couple months. She'd been like this for years. What if the damage was permanent?

"Dying," my mother said. "Dale Horowitz. Jennie Buck. Hal Klein. Of course they were all really sick. I told Stuart I was concerned. He said it was just a coincidence. 'Holly,' he said.

'Don't you worry about it. You did the best you could. Things happen.' So I tried. But I should have been there. You know people need something to live for. If they think it's hopeless, they just give up. That's why I worked my patients so hard. When you get back language, you feel empowered, you know."

I glanced at Casey, who shrugged and shook his head.

"Go on, Mom," he urged.

Mom pursed her lips. "I told your father that, too. Before the day he didn't come back. You know what he asked me? Did I trust Dr. Renfroe? I told him of course I did." She paused. Then she said, "I don't think your dad did, though. But then he was gone."

Her tone was so vacant, so detached. Could we buy any of this? She wasn't really Mom yet. The real Mom would be riled up that she hadn't pursued my father's hunch. At least that's what I hoped. Suddenly I thought back to that piece of sports column I'd kept. Of course Dad would have been suspicious. It was like what he'd said about baseball: If you were watching, you'd catch those tells. Those little signs.

He'd seen something in Renfroe. And so had we.

Jenna's Journal

December 9th
LATER THAT MORNING

When Amber arrived, Casey called me in absent from school. Then Amber pretended to be Mom and did the same for him.

In between the calls, Amber gave me a "lying is justified because there's a greater good involved" speech. The A-world continued to have a lot of gray areas, which was fine by me. I had never taken to the idea that Heaven was a bunch of folks who all thought the same way, sitting around, patting each other on the wings about their good fortune. On the other hand, it appeared even the more liberal angels weren't thrilled about my brother's inability to shake his marijuana habit.

All of which set me somewhere between happy and queasy. On top of everything else, I was now feeling comfortable (or close enough) with Amber Velasco. Maybe it would pass—like those ultra-skinny jeans everyone used to like until it occurred to most folks that unless you were anorexic or a heroin addict you pretty much looked like a sausage stuffed into a too-small casing.

I used Casey's phone to leave a message on Maggie's cell. She texted back immediately. *What the f is going on with you?*

I am not abbreviating. Maggie just typed 'f.' Unlike me and Amber and my brother, Maggie does not have a colorful vocabulary.

Mom's sick, I texted back, for lack of a better excuse.

Casey's phone buzzed almost as soon as I pressed send.

"Jenna?" Maggie made sure it was me and not Casey before she went on. "No offense, but your Mom is always sick. You need to get your butt to school. Do you need a ride or something?"

"Maybe by this afternoon," I said. "I'm gonna see how she feels."

We hung up. I knew she knew I was lying. It would have to wait.

I headed to Casey's room to find Amber eyeballing the two (yes, two) glass bongs sitting on the floor next to his laptop, the second being the rarely-used multi-colored one that Dave swore was imported from Germany. Instead of her perpetual EMT outfit (which she'd even worn bartending), she had on regular jeans and a long-sleeved black button-up shirt that showed a little cleavage and a hint of black lace bra. She was also wearing cowboy boots: a slick, pointy-toed pair that looked worn-in like she'd had them a while.

Casey was sitting on his bed, looking sheepish.

"What the hell am I doing here?" Amber said, mostly to herself.

"Please tell us!" I snapped. "We're dying to know!" I cringed, immediately regretting the lame pun and remembering the fact that Renfroe himself had used it.

Without an answer, she grabbed Casey's laptop, then sat at his desk and powered it on. I shuddered. If she wanted to touch his laptop, that was her business.

"Let's get to work," she said, adjusting her blouse around that lacy bra. There was no denying it. Outside her EMT gear and dorky utility belt, Amber Velasco was a hottie. Funny, if Casey weren't dead and practically back together with Lanie, he'd be in heaven right now. (Or not so funny.)

Amber's plan was to research every obituary we could find that connected to Oak View Convalescent Home.

"Let's start the day Dad disappeared," Casey suggested.

"I think we should start before that," Amber replied, her fingers flying over the keyboard. "Whatever this is, it has to be big. We have to find a pattern."

She had a point. If people were dying like my Mom had hinted, and the whole thing was bad enough to make my father disappear and cause Dr. Renfroe to mess with my mother's brain, we needed to cast a wide net. Not everyone who passed away got mentioned in the paper, of course. We got going and hoped for the best.

By nine in the morning, we'd found three people.

By ten, we'd found three more.

By noon, I'd snuck off for a quick shower and changed into jeans and my Ima Razorback shirt. Also my Converse, since unlike some people, I had no boots. I stopped to make tea and toast for Mom and lied to her about why I was home, claiming that it was a teacher work day. Oh, and I also ignored several texts on Casey's phone from Maggie.

By the time I returned to Casey's room at 12:30, he and Amber had uncovered four more deaths of elderly patients living at Oak View Convalescent. Most, but not all, seemed to have suffered from Alzheimer's. One guy had possibly died of a stroke. This was not an exact science; we had only the obituary wording and sometimes a request for contributions to go on. So if the family asked that in lieu of flowers, donations be made to Alzheimer research, we assumed that's what the person died of.

"Ten dead people," Casey said. "That's a lot, right?"

"It's a freaking old person's home!" I yelled.

He and Amber frowned at me.

"Old people die," I said. "It happens. Come on. I mean that's why they're there, right?" I wanted us to be wrong—about all of it. Was Dr. Renfroe really doing something to make all these old folks die before their time? Why? What sick reason could he possibly have?

Amber turned back to the screen. "Ten is ten too many. Even for a facility like that. None of the ten had cancer or any other immediately life-threatening illness or condition."

Casey began to pace back and forth. "So let's say Mom was on to something. What the hell is Dr. Renfroe doing over there? Knocking 'em off for sport? Feeding them poisoned tapioca pudding or something?"

"Not funny," I told him. "Remember me? Your poisoned sister?" I shifted my gaze to Amber's boots. If I still had boots, I would have shivered in them.

We tossed around possibilities. Dr. Renfroe was a crazed maniac. Dr. Renfroe had poisoned himself by accident and lost his mind. Dr. Renfroe owed the Mafia millions of dollars in gambling debts and was cashing in on phony insurance claims for his victims. (Amber's theory.) Dr. Renfroe was in fact a nice guy, but Oak View was built on Indian burial grounds and the ghosts were killing the residents. (Casey's theory. As far as I know, he hadn't touched either bong.) The patients were dying naturally, and this was all a crazy coincidence. (My theory.)

Somewhere in the middle of the theorizing, my stomach growled that it was finally ready to make up for lost time. "I'm *starving*," I announced. "Can you call over to Beijing Bistro?" Casey had baked the last frozen pizza for breakfast. Plus there was the definite possibility that Amber would pay for the food.

Amber's phone rang in her pocket. She glanced at the caller ID. "Terry," she mouthed to us: her friend at the lab.

Terry was a loud talker. Casey and I could hear most of it through the tinny phone speaker. We huddled around Amber. The herbal concoction in Mom's system—which we now knew was probably getting into her from the stash of vitamins helpfully supplied by Dr. Renfroe—was in fact what Terry had suspected. It had some of the properties of gingko biloba. But there was one big difference. It seemed to have the *opposite* effect. Terry wasn't sure why, but he aimed to find out.

Amber hung up and smiled at us. "Terry's a crazy man. He lives for this shit."

"What shit?" I demanded.

With that, Amber started jabbering like a girl with a crush. In the last 24 hours, Terry had also conducted a little experiment with mice. There were lots of lab mice at Texicon where he worked. Specifically, he'd given them the same chemical compound he'd discovered in Mom's blood. Then he sent them on a "memory course" to find cheese. Just a simple little maze that rodents could master easily. But instead of sharpening the mice memories—find the cheese, find the cheese—the compound made them forget the cheese. Stranger still, they didn't even seem to *care* about the cheese anymore. Maybe they knew it was there; maybe they didn't. But they walked right by it. If they bumped into it, maybe they would eat it. Maybe not.

All the talk about cheese made my stomach rumble.

"Meaning?" my brother asked.

Amber arched a perfect brow at us. "Meaning we have proof that Dr. Renfroe was giving your mother something to make her forget. On purpose. Now we need to find out why. And what it is he wanted her to forget. It had to do with the deaths at Oak View, I'm sure. But it's probably even bigger. When we know, I'm betting we'll know what happened to your father. Or at least we'll be closer to figuring it out. Terry's emailing over a PDF with the blood work specifics."

Then what? I wondered.

Would we just grab Renfroe and interrogate him? It wasn't like we were cops. This was not an episode of *Law & Order*. Besides, if it were, we'd be done by now and watching something else. Which would mean that we had dug up the truth, something I both wanted and didn't want all at once. A tiny piece of me still wanted to be wrong. I liked Renfroe. Up until three days ago, he seemed a decent guy. Plus, I was my father's daughter. I was pissed that I hadn't caught the tells.

Amber's phone beeped. The three of us huddled over the tiny screen again.

According to lab guru Terry, Mom's blood showed deficiencies in a bunch of the stuff that helps memory: B-12, folic acid, and E. Her good cholesterol was also crazy low; and Terry believed we needed to pump her up with omega-3 fatty acids (the phrase "fish oil" was repeated three times) and possibly a couple glasses of wine every day. He also suggested checking her teeth and making sure she didn't have a bladder infection.

In short: it was probable that Renfroe's so-called "vitamins" had been leeching everything good from my mother's system.

"Holy shit," Casey and I said together. We all agreed that: 1) Any colorful language was justified. 2) It was time for a road trip to visit Dr. Renfroe in his home turf of Oak View Convalescent Home. 3) We would pick up Chinese food on the way.

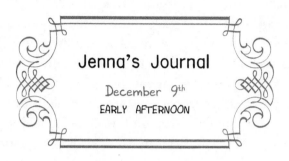

Jenna's Journal

December 9th
EARLY AFTERNOON

There was just one problem.

Now that the vitamins were working their way out of her system, Mom was starting to feel better.

There is only one good part (in my humble opinion) about having a mother who is totally unfocused and often slightly unhinged: Once you figure out how to ignore the fear and the anger and the not-knowing, you can basically do whatever you want. Your mother won't notice. But in the time between her tea and toast and our decision to head into Houston, Mom had started noticing.

"I know you must have told me," she said, "but why are you two home today?" She had moved to the couch in the family room and was drinking a mug of something (Tea? Hot water? We had no more coffee.) that she'd prepared all on her own. She was wearing jeans and a clean gray and white striped T-shirt and an old pair of topsiders. She'd arranged her hair into a half ponytail. There was pinkish lip gloss on her lips.

I stared at her. Casey stared at her. Amber stared at us.

Mom tilted her head. Her eyes looked sharper. Alert. This was amazing. This was fantastic. This was a nightmare.

"Teacher work day," I said. "Remember?"

The look that Mom gave me was the kind of look she should have been giving us for a long time now. The one that said she knew we were up to some youthful shenanigans. That she was on to us. That she would not ignore the sweet smell of pot wafting from her son's door night after night. That she would not just cry and go back to bed when her daughter passed out in front of her. *This* was the mom I had wanted so badly the past year. But now she had to go away. Now we needed to drive to the Medical Center and inform Dr. Renfroe that he was a slimy bastard who had made my father disappear, plied my mother with destructive vitamins, and most likely poisoned my boots for reasons unknown. Not to mention how he had probably killed off a bunch of innocent old folks.

"Amber?" Mom set her mug on the coffee table. "That's your name, right?"

Amber nodded anxiously.

"Why are you in my house in the middle of the day? Don't you have somewhere to be? Aren't you a paramedic? Is that your Mercury Marquis on our driveway?"

"Mom," Casey began. "Mom—"

"Jenna," my mother interrupted, turning to me.

"Yeah?"

Her forehead wrinkled, her eyes even more intense as she studied my face. "You've been sick, haven't you? And there was an accident. I . . ." She shifted back to Amber again.

"Mrs. Samuels." Amber's voice was soft but firm, her Texas twang more noticeable for some reason. "We think that Jenna may have been—"

The door bell rang.

All of us jumped. Even Mom. Amber opened up. For a horrified second, I thought it might be Renfroe, making an unannounced vitamin visit.

"I made Christmas fudge," announced Mrs. Gilroy. She held out a covered tin.

"Yum," Amber told her. "Smells delicious."

"Marshmallow Fluff," Mrs. Gilroy said. She poked her head in, peeking here and there like she was looking for something. "That's the secret ingredient. Are y'all doing an indoor decorating project?" she asked in a voice that let me know that's not what she thought. "Cause we think it might be draining your electric system or something and maybe leeching over to ours. Our manger scene just lit up all by itself. Weirdest thing."

None of us said a word. Mrs. Gilroy wasn't big on taking hints.

Amber snatched the tray from her. "Is that all, ma'am? Thanks so much."

She narrowed her eyes, but nodded. "You're looking better, Holly," she said to Mom on her way out.

Amber slammed the door. I realized for the millionth time how much we'd tried to hide what had been going on, and how it had sort of slipped out there anyway. How could I hide it? Especially from nosy asshat neighbors. Maybe I'd been looking for people to know. Looking for help even when I was telling myself that I didn't need any.

"Mom?" Casey asked.

I turned to her.

She was gone again. Just like that. The Gilroy's manger may have lit up, but that brief light in Mom's eye had flickered out. She asked Amber who she was again and Amber repeated, "I'm the EMT who helped Jenna and Casey. We talked last night, remember?"

Mom nodded, her attention scooting this way and that. "I'm sorry," she said. "I guess I do know, don't I?"

"Absolutely." Amber smiled.

It reminded me of when I was little—three or four maybe—and how I hated banana pudding even though the rest of the family loved it. Mom would make it and when I wrinkled my nose, she'd tell me, "You said last time that you liked it, Jenna." And I'd take a bite or two, believing her. It always took a few swallows before I realized I'd been duped. Mom was even more forgetful than that.

Casey helped her back to bed. Part of me wanted to tell her everything. Part of me didn't. And all of me knew that there were things she might never get to know. Things I did. Like how Casey hadn't exactly made it out of the accident. Mostly though, I felt impatient. We needed to get going. We needed to make sure that Mom stayed safe from now on. I watched as Casey settled Mom against the pillows and pressed two fingers gently to her forehead, keeping them there until Mom's eyes fluttered and began to shut.

"You rest now," he whispered.

Mom was already asleep.

A new worry surfaced. "Do you think it's permanent?" I asked Amber. "Even if she never takes a tainted vitamin again?" I didn't say the rest of it, the part where I wondered what would happen if Casey was gone for good, if we didn't find Dad, if I was left with a Mom who was still mostly incapacitated. I guessed that I would do what I'd been doing, only maybe better now that I wasn't dying from boot poison.

"We'll hope for the best," was what she said.

Right, I thought. Shit happens.

I wished she'd touched me when she'd said it. But she didn't.

I CLIMBED INTO the back of the Merc and let Amber ride shotgun. Mamaw Nell's photo was still lying on the backseat. I studied it as we headed to Houston.

"Here's what I still don't get." I eyeballed the image of Dr. Renfroe. He looked so sad and desperate. Even his chest hair looked sort of droopy. "We can prove that Dr. Renfroe gave Mom the vitamins. But we can't prove he knew what was in them, can we? And that's not even what's bothering me."

(Note: Lots of things were bothering me, including the fact that Casey had changed his mind about stopping for Chinese. Saying them out loud helped.)

I tried to put myself in Dr. Renfroe's place, but without the chest hair. He had done good work for people with serious health problems. But then what? Had he woken up one morning and decided to screw with old people, and then with my family? That could be true only if my mother had somehow stumbled on something going wrong at Oak View. We had placed him at the Isle of Capri in a snit. We had placed him at our house, visiting Mom and bringing her bottles of vitamins that had just about made her forget who she was.

On the other hand, he had taken care of me in the ER not once, but twice, and had diagnosed—correctly I hoped—the poison. He made me give up my damn boots to save my life. Unless of course, I took a turn for the worse.

"He's a smart dude," Casey said, with that unnerving new habit of saying the words that were forming in my brain. "I mean, you have to be pretty genius to fake a vitamin that takes away people's memories. The drug world would kill for something like that. A pill that makes people forget? That's why I started toking up in the first place. That and it feels good."

Amber flashed him a disgusted look: *Seriously?*

"What? When I'm high, I'm not worried. Unless I smoke too much. Then I get kind of paranoid, although not as much as Dave." Here Casey paused, probably because he was remembering that Dave's marijuana-induced paranoia about the flashing Prius dash display was how the Prius got smashed the first time.

"Wait a second," said Amber. "Go back—"

"Dave's an idiot," I told her. "Don't worry about it."

"Not that," Amber muttered impatiently. "This. Why would a doctor who works with people who are already losing their memories create a drug that would make them forget?"

"It doesn't make sense," I agreed. "How long does it take to create a new drug?"

"Depends on what kind," Casey said. I guess hanging out with Dave gave him some expertise. "People cut stuff into marijuana all the time. But actual drugs that you prescribe to people—that takes years. There are tests and trials and it has to get approved by the FDA. That's why people get so upset sometimes with stuff like cancer drugs. If you're sick, you want the cure right away. You don't want to wait five years for it to be tested because you might not have five years."

Amber nodded in the front seat. "Exactly. I'm happy to see you're not stoned right now."

It was like a knee-jerk thing with her, being all bossy. Casey flashed me a fed-up look in the rearview mirror.

He checked behind us and changed lanes to merge with Highway 59 and then 288 to the Med Center, spread out

block after block with tons of hospitals and rehab centers and smaller specialized places like Oak View.

"Okay," I said. "If Dr. Renfroe somehow created a drug that made people forget—which is totally illogical but let's go with it—it's not something he'd come up with spur of the moment. So even if he wanted to hurt Mom's memory because she knew something was fishy about him, it's not like he could just create a pill for that overnight."

"Your father's been gone for five years," Amber countered. "I'm sorry. That came out harsher than I meant."

I wasn't offended. Amber the Annoying was right. I glanced at the photo again, forcing myself to concentrate, to make everything click into place. Even if he was a twisted psychopath—and several signs pointed that way—Renfroe, unlike two of the people in the car with me, was still human. He was smart, yes—genius, maybe—but not Einstein genius. The facts we knew for sure: he was a hairy guy who ran a convalescent home and moonlighted in the ER. How could *he* possibly have created a miracle memory-erasing drug?

Miracle.

Something in my head shifted. My own lights lit up. In English class last year we learned Greek mythology. The ancient Greeks believed that the Goddess Athena sprang out of her dad Zeus's head fully grown. Athena. Goddess of Wisdom. When the thought I was trying to form finally squeezed its way out of my brain and onto my tongue, that's how it felt. Like Athena popping out of my head.

"Listen!" I poked between the two front seats. "Think about it. The guy doesn't have enough hours in the day to make a memory drug just for Mom. So what does that mean? It means that he already had the drug. But it means more than that. There's probably no way he would have purposely come up with something to *hurt* memory. That's goofy, right? He'd want something that would *help* it. Even I remember Mom talking about that kind of stuff before she lost it, how doctors are creating drugs all the time to improve short- and long-term memory. That's what everyone wants with Alzheimer's right? The miracle cure."

"Holy crap," Casey said. Oak View was just down the block, but he slammed the brakes so fast my stomach lurched. My body remembered the panic when we'd crashed the Prius. The Merc slowed to a stop, its right tires scraping the curb. He angled in his seat and looked at me. "That's it," he whispered, his eyes pulsating. "He wanted to get rich off making people *remember*. That's why there was gingko whatever in the drug."

"Which means," Amber said, in a voice that was pure East Texas high-pitched excitement, "that maybe something went wrong. And maybe the reason all those people have been dying is because he tried it out on them. He took a gamble. We know he's the gambling kind."

I had to smile. "Exactly." I waved the photo. "Look at him. People like Mamaw Nell go to gamble because it's fun. They don't mind losing a little cash. It's just an afternoon of slots. But what if you were really desperate? What if you lost a bunch of money and wanted to get it back?"

Both Casey and Amber nodded, waiting for me to go on.

I couldn't. That was all I had. We weren't quite there, but we were on to something.

"Okay, here's another thought," Casey said quietly, "What if Dad knew, too? Dad was a journalist. He might have been doing sports reporting, but what if he decided to investigate something Mom had tipped him off to? Or even something he was doing secretly behind her back, to protect

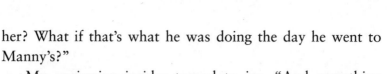

her? What if that's what he was doing the day he went to Manny's?"

My squirming insides turned to ice. "And something went wrong," I said. "So Renfroe tests a memory drug on his patients. Only it makes them forget. Or makes them sick and eventually dead. What if whatever he was putting in them, he forced on Dad? And then put in Mom's vitamins?"

"I have an idea," Amber said. "Wait a second." She pulled out her cell. "Either of you know the Oak View number?"

We both knew it by heart. She pressed it into her cell.

Casey and I held our breath.

"Hello," Amber said in the sweetest of voices. "I need to speak to the office manager, please." She waited. Then she started talking again, her drawl slower now and so sweet it made my molars twitch. "This is Lara Jean Simpkins over at Chase Bank. We've found some discrepancies in the Oak View Convalescent account records that we need to discuss with y'all. I'm sending a bank examiner out your way. I've already been in contact with Dr. Renfroe. He told me you're the one who's in charge. Said you'd be happy to chat. Yes, that's Simpkins with an s on either end. Thanks so much. The examiner's name is Rodney Baker. He'll be there within an hour."

She hung up and shoved the phone back into her jeans pocket. Then she smiled at the both of us.

"You're good," Casey told her.

"Pull up some, but not all the way to the parking lot," Amber directed, all business again. "We need to be able to see the driveway. If I'm right, it won't be long."

Not ten minutes later, Dr. Renfroe's shiny black Audi shot out of the Oak View lot, hung a right, and barreled down the block.

Three Things I Now Know About Tailing Someone Near Oak View:

1) It stinks if you are driving in a car the size of a medium motor boat, with the get-up-and-go of a horse and buggy.

2) The neighborhood has a lot of twists and turns. It would have helped if we were chasing a slower car than an Audi. (Dr. Renfroe should have moonlighted as a NASCAR driver instead of an ER doctor and/or psychopath.)

"SHOULD WE CALL the cops?" I asked.

We were chugging a few cars behind Renfroe, who—(for reasons unknown) was now headed uptown. The Galleria Mall loomed ahead.

"And tell 'em what?" Casey executed a sharp left across traffic as the Audi scooted into the Galleria underground parking lot.

I stifled a yelp. The place was jammed with cars. Three weeks before Christmas, after all. If Renfroe was looking for a space, this was going to take awhile.

"The truth," Amber said. "Well, not all of it. They wouldn't believe it. Let's see what he's up to first. When we've got proof, yes, we need to involve the cops."

I took two things from this. The first was that Amber seemed to have a plan to bring the guilty parties to justice. The second was that she was *right*. People were strange. They believed all sorts of stupid crap. They fell for Internet scams asking to save Nigerian princes. Watched reality TV like it was real. But if I walked up to that knot of Christmas shoppers standing at the entrance to Nordstrom's, and I told them I'd sped here in Mamaw Nell's borrowed Mercury Marquis in hot pursuit of a man whose miracle drug had gone wrong and had attempted to destroy my family, they would gawk at me like the lunatic I appeared to be. And that was *leaving out* the angel part.

We tailed the Audi around and around the packed garage. Up two floors, down two floors, this way and then that in the aisles of cars. Was it always this crowded? Truth was: I hadn't been to a mall in a while, not since before Halloween, any-way. Finally Renfroe slowed to a stop. A Range Rover pulled out, leaving a vacant spot.

"Follow him, Amber," Casey said. "I'll figure something out." I kept my eye on the Audi, hoping that Renfroe was so focused on going wherever he was going that he wouldn't look our way. There was no mistaking Mamaw Nell's Merc.

"Stay with your brother," Amber commanded. She leaped from the car and crouched low between a BMW sedan and a Honda.

Screw this. I was out of the Merc and squatting next to her before either of them could protest.

"Get back in the car!" Amber hissed. She hunkered lower as the driver's door of the Audi swung open.

I peered around the BMW's fender. Dr. Renfroe straightened. He glanced behind him nervously, but didn't seem to spot the Merc. I held my breath and withdrew my head. The Merc idled, exhaust fumes billowing up my nose. Any second now I was going to break into a coughing fit. Amber peeked over the Honda. When she sighed, I knew Renfroe had entered the Galleria.

She glared down at me. "If you're coming, then c'mon. We don't want to lose him." She slapped the Merc's trunk like she was hitting the rear end of a horse. "Go!" she shouted in my brother's general direction. "Text me when you're inside."

Amber took off at a race walk, her pointy-toed boots slapping the concrete. I chased, my Converse soles a lame squeak in comparison.

"Don't you just know?" I hollered.

She gave me the stink eye over her shoulder. "Know what?"

"Know where Renfroe is. Where he's going. Like with Casey. You know where he is all the time—"

"You're kidding, right?" she spat. She pushed through the doors into the brightly lit mall. Christmas assailed us: silver and white snowflakes, a display of ginormous gold ornaments, red and green "50% OFF!" banners, a grouping of life-sized nutcrackers, all in a backdrop of glittering store windows and faux marble flooring. I felt woozy. Amber picked up the pace. I spotted Renfroe's curly dark hair ahead of us, near the Starbucks kiosk.

"Don't let him see you," she whispered.

Casey better get in here pretty quick. Otherwise Detective

Bossy and I were going to end up throwing down in front of
Armani.

Dr. Renfroe moved briskly into the vast atrium, past the
giant Christmas tree in the middle toward the bank of eleva-
tors at the far end. He pressed the up button. I heard Amber's
cell buzz in her pocket. Casey.

"Ten to one he's headed upstairs in the Financial Center," she told my brother. "We're right behind him."

I tapped her on the shoulder. "Shouldn't we—"

"Wait," Amber snapped, not bothering to let me finish.

I returned that stink eye. But I waited.

Renfroe stepped into an elevator. The door closed. Amber
crept closer, gesturing for me to follow. She raised a finger to
her lips and pointed towards the upper levels with her other
hand: six levels that ringed the atrium and the big, fat, too-
tall Christmas tree smack in the middle. I squinted in the
glare of the skylight.

"Fifth floor, if I'm right," she whispered. "Wait for it."

Was she listening for something? Because all I could
hear was a bunch of eager-beaver Christmas shoppers
with way too much time and money on their hands. That,
and the faint muzak strains of "Jingle Bell Rock" echoing
from every direction. I tried to follow her eyes, counting
upwards.

All at once, she grabbed my hand. She dragged me to the
elevator bank.

When the door opened, Amber whipped her EMT badge
from her back pocket. "Out!" she demanded of the crowd
inside.

There was a slight murmur. It was holiday time, and the
way I figured it, people were already irritable with the need
to pretend that they were happy. Plus Amber was dressed in

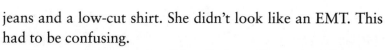

jeans and a low-cut shirt. She didn't look like an EMT. This had to be confusing.

"You really authorized?" asked a tall guy in a business suit and cowboy boots.

"Do I need to call someone?" Amber asked him right back.

Everybody hustled out, double-time.

Amber jabbed the 5 button and the doors slid shut. Up we went. One. Two. Three. Four . . . The doors slid open. Quieter up here, except for one loud shouting voice. My blood ran cold. I knew that voice. We stepped out. On the other side of our ring, across the vast empty expanse of the atrium, Renfroe was shouting at two men.

Two very familiar men.

One was tall and thin, with a shaved bald head. Manny, of Manny's Tex Mex: the last place my father had been seen alive, five years ago. The other guy was shorter and muscular, with hairy arms sticking out of his short sleeved shirt. I didn't know his name. It didn't matter. He'd waited on me. Or tried. He'd been royally pissed that I was part of a party of four who'd only ordered for one—that crucial *one* being Zeke, Bryce's friend, the Zeke who never forgot a face or a fact.

So here I was, staring at Manny, Hairy-Armed Waiter, and Dr. Renfroe, hollering at each other in front of some office at the top of the Galleria.

Amber punched the key pad of her cell. "Where the hell are you?" she muttered tightly.

I assumed she'd called Casey. When she didn't say anything else, I assumed he hadn't answered. With one eye on Renfroe and the others, I watched as she switched to texting.

5ᵗʰ floor she typed.

She shoved the phone back into her pocket. Then she started cussing to herself in a decidedly non-holy being fashion. The colorful language was directed mostly at my brother. I didn't catch the specifics, though. Being here felt a lot like the car accident, when the Prius was tumbling and all I could think was that I couldn't think at all.

"Hey! Amber! Jenna!" Casey's voice poked into my ears from somewhere below. He shouted louder. "Hey! I'm here!"

I turned to the Renfroe gang.

My heart froze. Casey stood directly below them—on floor four, not floor five. He waved at us across the open air of the atrium, clutching a Bath and Body gift bag in his hand. My brain did some quick mental gymnastics.

This much was obvious: Casey had no clue that Dr. Renfroe, Manny, and Hairy-Armed Waiter were standing on the floor above him. Additionally, he had stopped to shop. I began to seethe. I was not the only teenage girl who enjoyed the skin-smoothing product line at Bath and Body. (You'd be a moron not to. Mags gave me one of their vanilla lotions as a birthday gift last year. She knew I couldn't afford it. I was a boot-wearing girl, but that didn't mean I wasn't concerned with proper skin care.) No, I'd be willing to gamble that Lanie Phelps did, too. Not that I was the gambling kind. In short: Casey was late to our hot pursuit of Dr. Renfroe because he had stopped to Christmas or date (or both) shop for his possibly no longer ex-girlfriend. Which meant he just possibly might have indulged in a smidgen of cannabis to calm himself.

Why else would he be waving at us like an idiot? At least he was *here*. Maybe someday Ryan Sloboda would stop in the middle of a life and death crisis to buy me a present. It could happen. I decided to cut my brother some slack. Although I

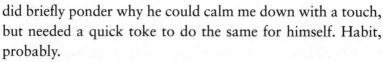

did briefly ponder why he could calm me down with a touch, but needed a quick toke to do the same for himself. Habit, probably.

Hairy-Armed Waiter leaned far over the railing. "Hey!" he shouted down to Casey.

Dr. Renfroe and Manny stepped up beside him. They spotted Amber and me at the same time.

"Stop!" Amber shouted. "Stay right there!"

I almost laughed at what happened next. It didn't seem real in the least. Hairy Arms whipped a pistol out of the back of his jeans. From where I was standing, maybe thirty yards across, it looked like a plastic water gun. Then he aimed at us. I heard the whizzing even before I heard the firecracker pop. Plaster from the wall behind us fluffed out like a little perfume spray.

Amber slammed me to the floor and flopped on top of me. I bit my tongue. There was blood in my mouth.

"He's shooting at us?" I gasped.

"Just shut up and stay still," Amber grunted, shielding me with her body.

I peeked through the railing. Casey had vanished. Dr. Renfroe was now wrestling with Hairy Arms. Manny was trying to pull them apart. With a violent yank, Renfroe pulled the gun from the waiter's hands. But the gun kept sailing up in midair, free now from all three of them. It bounced on the railing and then over into the empty air of the atrium. I cringed, praying it wouldn't hit some poor shopper on the head. There was a faint metallic smack as it hit the ground floor.

Seconds later, a rumble of people started shouting from below.

"We have to get out of here," Amber whispered.

I nodded.

We stood up, only to find ourselves facing a very sweaty Renfroe, Manny, and Hairy-Armed Waiter, sprinting around the circular balcony straight towards us. Amber glanced at me. She looked as scared as I felt. For the first time since I'd met her, I understood chaos theory. Shit happens. You deal with it.

"If you want to kill us, fine!" I heard myself shout. "But just tell me why."

At that, Renfroe stopped in his tracks. Hairy-Armed Waiter spun around and glared at him. Manny kept his beady eyes pinned to us, his scrawny lungs heaving.

"I had to," Renfroe choked out. He wiped his dripping, pale face with the back of his hand. A vein throbbed in his forehead. "They made me. Manny found out that your dad was still alive. He—"

"Shut up, Stuart," Manny barked.

"Oh God," Renfroe croaked. "I was trying to help. I was trying to help." He shot a furtive stare at Amber and me, then bolted for the balcony's edge.

Only when he grabbed the railing did I realize what he was about to do.

The rest seemed to happen in slow motion. I lunged for his ankles. The momentum of his jump pulled me over with him.

"Jenna!" I heard Casey scream from somewhere below.

Stuart Renfroe and I somersaulted through the air.

The Christmas tree spun below us, the skylight spun above us: a dazzling spiral. We'd left the balcony far behind. My stomach shrunk as we plunged. I squeezed my eyes shut. Weirdly, I felt something not unlike that peaceful feeling that I'd felt whenever Casey or Amber had touched or held me for

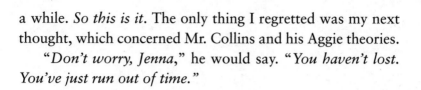

a while. *So this is it.* The only thing I regretted was my next thought, which concerned Mr. Collins and his Aggie theories.

"*Don't worry, Jenna,*" he would say. "*You haven't lost. You've just run out of time.*"

Jenna's Journal

December 10th
MORNING

W hat happened next was, in fact, a real-life miracle.
Of course, the possibility of miracles probably
increases if you're already hanging out with angels.

I'd rather not think too hard about all that right now.
Back to what happened:

Much later that night, after we found out why Renfroe
had done it (which I'll get to in a minute), Casey and I sat
cross-legged on his floor, the laptop between us. The You-
Tube videos were already starting to go viral. From one angle
or another, all of them showed a record crowd of Christmas
shoppers at the Houston Galleria, thrilled and mesmerized by
an unannounced show of two daredevil indoor stunt-people
with wing-shaped parachutes and angel costumes.

"I don't freaking believe it," Casey said with a chuckle.
"Let's watch that last one again."

I rested my hand on my brother's shoulder. "Casey," I
said. "Are you—?"

"Shh," he whispered. He threw his arm around my

shoulder and squeezed me against him. "Just one more time."

Casey started the video again. I watched, remembering, or trying to remember from my perspective. This particular clip had spliced together two different views, one of me and Renfroe hurtling over the balcony, the other of Casey leaping after us even before his wings unfurled. I could see why spectators bought the story that he was an indoor sky diver. How else could they explain that he'd been free-falling and then suddenly soared through the air over a giant Christmas tree?

The video switched back to my side of the Galleria. By the time Casey's wings had popped out and open, Amber had leaped over the edge, too. So there it was: Amber, wings spread wide, glowing like a thousand candles, swooping after Dr. Renfroe, who had managed to wrestle his ankles from my grip. She scooped him up and rose so gracefully that even this close to the screen, I couldn't see her wings flap. She set Dr. Renfroe in front of the security guards, now swooping (wingless) in on Hairy-Armed Waiter and Manny.

Renfroe's face was glowing hot red now. The audio on this clip wasn't the best, but I could hear him start spouting his confession. The same stuff he eventually wrote out for the cops once they hauled his sorry ass to jail.

Of course, I didn't remember any of this. All I remembered was hurtling through the air, then lying in Casey's arms as he laid me down. I was certain I must have been dead, because I could see his enormous, beautiful wings flapping.

Now, watching it play out on video, I saw how Casey dropped Lanie's package, the Bath and Body bag all wrapped up tight with pretty red ribbon and a card dangling from it. He just dove. It vanished in an instant as the camera followed

us. If he hadn't stopped to buy it, maybe he wouldn't have been there when I needed him.

"Jesus H. Christ," my brother whispered for the millionth time, reaching over to press replay. I sniffed the tiniest bit of weed on his otherwise fresh-as-a-daisy breath. "What the hell did you think you were doing, Jenna?"

"Saving the day," I whispered back. "Just like you."

I bit my lip, not wanting to ask the natural next question, given what Amber had told us about wings and A-words. (Was I ready to say angels yet? Maybe I was.)

Casey smiled, his eyes still on the screen. "I'm not going anywhere, Jenna. I just used up my earthly flight is all."

"How do you know?" I asked. I was worried I might start crying.

Casey shrugged. "I don't. Look, all I care about right now is that Mom has slept through this whole freaking insanity. Can you imagine what she's gonna say?"

I tried to laugh, but my eyes moistened. "Stop trying to change the subject. What if you need them again? What if I need them? What if—"

Casey's cell rang. When he answered, I could hear Lanie shouting from her end. "I saw you on the news! Was that really you? Since when have you become a stuntman?"

I decided to leave him alone then and get some sleep, too. I reminded myself that with or without boots, I was a Texas girl. I would take things as they came.

IT WAS A good thing that Amber Velasco—EMT, bartender, and maybe not so annoying angel—preferred cleavage-showing shirts, body hugging jeans, and kick-ass pointed boots. Because when she'd sashayed into the police station that same night to do a little recon, she was able to convince them not to press charges for the "indoor skydiving stunt." It had certainly not been authorized by the Galleria, and the Galleria owners were extremely pissed off. Somehow, she was able to convince them that she and Casey and I were in fact "indoor skydivers." In other words, a bunch of young idiots wandering around on the fifth floor of the Galleria looking for a place to do our stunt, when we happened to run into a bunch of crooks. And since those crooks recognized Casey and me, well, the extraordinary series of coincidences paid off.

The kicker? She was also able to finagle a copy of Renfroe's confession. It was scrawled in his own shaky handwriting, and without any prompting, apparently. The guy had a lot to get off his hairy chest. Amber appeared at our door with it just about sunrise. Mom was still asleep, thankfully. The three of us retreated to Casey's room and sat on the bed in a row, reading together as Amber flipped the pages.

All I ever wanted was to improve memory for my patients. The FDA wasn't moving fast enough. They never do. I was on the verge of a cure for Alzheimer's! They should have jumped at the chance. How many people in this country would give everything they have not to watch someone they love waste away? But instead the government kept testing.

So, yes. I did a preliminary trial on my own. I didn't have any other choice. I'm not crazy. I was helping. Can't you see that? Sometimes there's collateral damage. I didn't mean for it to go so far. You have to believe that.

No one died at first. If someone had died, ████████ I would have stopped, even if I knew that I would succeed down the line. But I was working on my own and I had to keep it quiet. Secrecy wasn't that hard to maintain, because nobody on my staff questioned what I was doing, except for one person. Holly Samuels was the X factor in my whole equation. She was the only one who mentioned the meds I seemed to be giving to patients that didn't come straight from a pharm company.

Then her husband Mike started asking around, too.

If she had minded her own business, it all would have worked out. But she didn't. I respected Holly Samuels. I trusted Holly Samuels. But I couldn't have her ruining everything.

In the first round of baseline testing, ████████ five patients regained most of their short-term memory when ingesting the drug I called M1. At first I was elated. But a week into that first trial, their other cognitive functions began fading. It's a common problem with memory-enhancing drugs: You gain in one spot and you lose in another. The brain is tricky that way. I don't mean any disrespect, but this is something the law enforcement community and legislature will never understand.

Back to the sequence of events, as you've asked me to transcribe: As I continued testing, they began to forget more. By the ▬▬▬▬▬ tenth trial dose, they forgot the things most important to them, even their names. I knew I had to work harder. No good in remembering what you ate for breakfast if you can't remember your children. So I re-configured the chemical compounds but something went wrong. One patient died. But he was 88. He had a heart condition.

Then another died. And another. And ten more after that.

I was and still am convinced I could crack the secret. I couldn't stop. I was too far in debt. I'd been a poker player since college, great at figuring the odds. It made no sense to me. Patients were dying and I was losing at cards. I tried to make it up at blackjack and slots. No use. I'd lost the touch. But you have to understand, I was sure I'd get it back. Luck turns. Things change. And I was trying to do something good.

Right around the same time I re-mortgaged Oak View to cover my losses, I met Manny. It wasn't a coincidence. Manny isn't just the enchilada king. He's connected. He keeps an office in the Galleria, so that should be a huge tip-off. How could the owner of a Tex-Mex restaurant afford such swank real estate?

He never told me who his partners were. I never asked. When someone can recite your bank statements verbatim, you shut the hell up. Manny trolls for people like me, people whose fortunes take a turn for the worse, so he can blackmail them. It's that simple.

But I was a special case. And there's a simple reason for that, too: My mistake was worth more to Manny and his

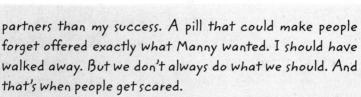

partners than my success. A pill that could make people forget offered exactly what Manny wanted. I should have walked away. But we don't always do what we should. And that's when people get scared.

So when I overheard Holly Samuels on the phone with her husband, talking about dying patients and weird symptoms, I gave into fear. She'd been watching me when she thought I wasn't looking. But it wasn't that. It was that her husband was a journalist.

What would Manny's men do if they found out an employee was on to me, that her journalist husband was nosing around Oak View? Fear's a funny thing. I had never been afraid like that. My logic: if I got rid of Mike, Holly would be so grief-stricken that she wouldn't care about Oak View anymore.

So I called Mike to set up a meeting, to talk about his wife's suspicions. I made one condition: he keep our meeting a secret. I almost lost my nerve, but Manny and his boys were watching. They set it all up: the waitress and the spill, so he'd have to take a trip to the men's room, where I was waiting with a needle. After the injection, Mike Samuels promptly forgot who he was. I'd gotten <u>that</u> good at synthesizing a drug that destroyed the very thing I wanted to save. I'm not boasting. I'm being honest. Manny and his boys were proud. Ask them, if they don't kill you first.

That's the whole point. I couldn't do what Manny really wanted. I couldn't kill the guy. So I dumped him on a Grayhound bus and sent him off to LA with no ID in his wallet. If he wasn't mugged or arrested, something else would happen.

Of course, Holly came to work the next day hysterical. Mike hadn't come home. He'd left a note on the counter, but he wasn't answering his cell phone. What would she tell Casey and Jenna? What was she going to do?

That first day, I was sure she was manipulating me, trying to get me to confess. Fear consumed me. Of course Mike had told her about our meeting. But as the weeks went on, I realized he hadn't. My plan was working. Holly was in no condition to be suspicious of me anymore.

You know what I didn't count on? The guilt.

I started funneling money into Holly's bank account. I didn't want her kids to starve. I'm not a bad man. One of my casino acquaintances knew how to make online transactions without leaving a trail. I never added too much. Just enough to keep them from losing everything.

But eventually the fear came back. Holly Samuels was a smart woman. Not as smart as I am, but smart enough. She'd say something to those kids of hers. Jenna was too young, but the boy—Casey—he was sharp. What if he began to see the connections? By then the police had almost convinced her that her husband didn't want to be found.

I hated seeing her look so sad and defeated, but that's the way it had to be.

And that's the way it stayed for about four years. Time slips by faster than you think. Especially when you're looking over your shoulder, making sure you're not about to get caught. My life ceased to be my own. I was a slave to Manny and his boys. Gambling away the money they gave me on the drug I created to make their victims forget. Some life, huh? I'm a caring guy, you see. That's what I'm trying to tell you. Sometimes Holly still cried when she thought no one was looking.

Then about a year ago, Holly dropped a bomb on me. She was suddenly determined to find Mike's body, because she

was convinced he was dead. "I know I was wrong," she told me that day. "Mike might leave me. But he'd never leave the kids. I'm thinking about hiring a private detective."

That day, I stopped funding their bank account. Two days later, I began supplying Holly with her vitamins. I told her daughter to make sure her mother took her medicine. That might have been the end of it. But the thought of Mike out there kept needling at my brain. What if he was alive? What if his memory had returned? What if he'd figured everything out and was watching us, just waiting for the right moment to strike and get us all? Like I said: fear makes you crazy.

Then Manny confirmed those worst fears for me. Mike Samuels was out there, all right. Not just out there. Close. In Texas. Working as a groundskeeper at a ballpark for some rinky-dink minor league team, the Round Rocks.

I might not be remembering that correctly, by the way. I was too terrified to remember anything clearly. Besides, Manny might have been lying. ▬▬▬▬▬▬▬▬▬

At first I'd planned to poison Holly, to use her as bait.

But Jenna's boots were lying on the living room floor. Every time I ever saw that girl she was wearing those boots, except for this one day. Maybe that's why I made the spot decision. It was dumb luck. No father could resist coming to rescue his daughter.

While Holly was in the bathroom, I spiked the inner soles of those boots with the poison I'd intended to use on Holly. My plan was to make Mike Samuels come out of hiding. And that's all I can tell you.

I don't know what happened at the Galleria. But I suspect it's the beginning of a process I deserve and have had long coming.

Dr. Stuart Renfroe, MD

~⁀

"JUST LIKE YOU guys suspected," Amber said, folding the papers and handing them to Casey, who then handed them to me.

"You should have dropped him," Casey said. His voice was low and I could see his jaw tighten. "You should have let the bastard die."

I reached across Amber and patted his thigh. "No wonder he made the miracle snake venom diagnosis," I said. "He'd given it to me. Of course he knew what it was." Guess that was one way to interpret that Hippocratic Oath. I blinked several times. My eyes were stinging. There was suddenly a lump in my throat the size of a baseball, but I choked out: "Dad might be in Texas."

"Exactly," Amber said. "I wanted to show you this first before I told you the rest. I talked to some of my cop friends at the station. Friends through Terry." She flushed and glowed a little.

(Note to self: If Terry wasn't to Amber what Lanie was to Casey, he was pretty damn close.)

"Anyway." She took a deep breath and stood, turning to face the both of us. "They've found someone matching his description, with his name, in Austin. But they haven't contacted him yet."

The room spun dizzily. I clutched at the bedspread.

Casey just kept shaking his head. "So why hasn't he come home yet?" he asked in a small voice.

That was a good question. But I could tell by the silence the three of us had already guessed the answer. Dad really *had* forgotten about us.

"We need to go to Austin," I said.

Amber nodded.

"Yeah," Casey said, "except for one thing."

"What?"

"Mom. You still can't tell her about me. Can't tell Dad either, if we find him."

I was about to argue, but stopped. "Okay," I said. I wiped my eyes and straightened. That preacher at Maggie's church, the one who had talked about slippery slopes and telling the truth, had also told us about forgiveness. You can't move on until you forgive, he said. When it came to Dr. Renfroe—who had smashed our family into crooked bits—I had a feeling I'd be stuck for awhile.

But I didn't want Mom to be stuck, too. Not any more than she already was.

So yes, I would keep Casey's secret from her. And I knew right then that I'd also keep Renfroe's. I would never tell her that he changed his mind at the last minute and poisoned me instead of her. I didn't give a damn if Mom ever forgave Renfroe. But I knew as sure as I knew anything that she would never forgive herself, not for what happened to either Casey or me. Even if it wasn't her fault, she would still feel responsible. That's what parents did.

At least parents whose brains hadn't been scrambled.

Jenna's Journal

December 18th

Maggie and I exchanged Christmas gifts early. I told her I was going on a road trip to Austin and I wasn't sure when we'd be back. Maggie made me open hers first: a black tank top with an array of sparkles and sequins on the top that she'd designed herself. I almost choked on my own spit when I realized the design was of an angel.

"Don't know why I thought of that for you," she said. "But I was arranging the sequins and suddenly there it was. Not too hokey?"

I hugged her tight. "Perfect," I said. "Really."

She unwrapped my gift to her. Presents were tricky. We were still broke, although Mom had started applying for jobs. Oak View had closed for now, but the Med Center was a big place. Hopefully someone would be in need of a speech therapist who was now a specialist on memory issues. But in all honesty, we had no idea if Mom would ever be totally herself again. I guess none of us would.

"Yum!" Maggie said. "And also perfect!" I had given her

two gifts: a pack of press-on tattoos of famous artists (the Van Gogh tattoo had only one ear) and a tin of homemade snickerdoodles. Mamaw Nell had shared her recipe.

When she asked why we were going to Austin, I replied, "A change of pace."

It wasn't the truth, but it was hardly a lie.

AT FIRST WE didn't tell Mom why we were going to Austin, either.

Casey and I met Amber for kolaches to discuss a possible ruse. Amber had already staked out a table at the doughnut shop when we arrived, a huge box at her feet.

"For you," she told me.

The label read Bubba's Boot Town.

Inside was a shiny new pair of Ariats, pointy-toed like Amber's. They were red and tan leather, and the inside was lined with blue.

"Texas girls need their boots," Amber said. "Besides, it's high time you returned those borrowed purple clogs to Nurse Ed."

Of all the things I'd ever expected from Amber Velasco, I had never expected her to make me cry. I swallowed, hard. I tried to think of funny things. It didn't work.

"Thanks," I croaked. The boots fit just right: tight at the instep and giving a little at the heel. Cow leather, not snakeskin, which was fine by me. She had also included a bottle of leather conditioner. My feet felt like dancing. If I had been Amber, I'd have spread my wings and flown around Sundale Donuts in happiness. Instead, I scarfed two sausage kolaches and sucked down a container of chocolate milk.

"So here's what I'm thinking," Casey began. "We—"

His phone rang. When he checked the caller ID, his eyes lit up.

Amber heaved a sigh. "Go ahead. Get this out of your system."

Casey made no comment, just hightailed it out of the doughnut shop, his cell already clapped to his ear.

"Want to split this last one?" Amber pointed to the remaining sausage kolache. All of a sudden I noticed that she was back in her EMT outfit today.

"You really are an EMT?" I asked. Yes, I trusted Amber Velasco now. But I also knew that she would never tell us the whole truth if she could help it, about anything.

Amber shrugged. "More or less."

I frowned.

"Like your brother going to school still." She slurped some more coffee. Pressed her finger to the kolache crumbs on the napkin and licked them off. "It's a cover. I'm a part-timer when it suits my purposes. Right now, it does."

I kept frowning. "That's it?"

She flashed a half-smile. "Jenna, come on."

I glanced out the window at Casey, blabbing on his cell, as happy as I'd ever seen him. Did he not know that the whole Lanie thing was never going to work out? Or maybe it was. That was the problem. I just didn't know. About Lanie. About how long Casey would stay here. About the wings and how he'd used up his flight saving me. But Amber had used hers up, too, hadn't she?

And that's when it happened: everything that I still didn't know came burbling up and out. Question after question after question . . .

Amber didn't look upset in the least. She folded her arms across her chest as I spilled. When I was finally done, I took a deep breath and flopped back in my seat. She stared at me for few long beats without saying anything. Then she glanced wistfully out the window at Casey.

"Everything you overheard at Mario's is true," she said. "I mean, you want to know about me, right? I was living with my boyfriend. It was my senior year and I'd just finished my med-school applications. Someone broke into our apartment one night . . ." Amber stopped talking. Her gaze went somewhere that I couldn't go.

"Were you in love with him? Your boyfriend?"

"Yeah," Amber said. "I was." She eyeballed Casey again, then shifted her gaze back at me.

I leaned forward. "And is he still alive? Is he—"

"He's not an angel," Amber said, "if that's what you want to know."

What I wanted was the rest of the story. What had happened to her? Who had done it? What had happened to her boyfriend? Was it Terry? How had she ended up with wings? But I understood that this was all I was getting. At least for now.

"I'll tell you something else," she said. She wrapped her hands around her Styrofoam cup of coffee. Lowered her voice. Her perfect bangs looked just the tiniest bit flatter today, tired out. "Something your brother doesn't know. I'd rather you not tell him, but I'll leave that up to you."

I nodded.

"I know I should have, but I didn't give a rat's ass whether Renfroe killed himself. He's not why I flew out there, Jenna. Justice or no justice. Anyone who could do what he did, no matter what his reasons . . . I flew to catch you, Jenna." She raised the cup to her lips, then set it down without taking a drink. "But when I saw that Casey was

already one step ahead of me, I had to make a choice. Your brother was going to suffer for what he did either way. He was already out there, already committed. There was no turning back. So I did what I had to. I let him come for you and I grabbed up Renfroe instead. Might as well get some benefit out of it since I'd already taken the leap. Jenna, your brother might have lost his chance to fly while here on Earth. But he did it to save you. I needed to let him have that."

My cheeks were suddenly wet. I sniffed and nodded again. *Thanks,* I mouthed.

You're welcome, she mouthed back.

The Aggie 12th Man, I thought. That was Amber Velasco. Even if she and Casey were now effectively benched with the wing debacle. She was there no matter what.

Casey burst back into the shop, grinning from ear to ear. "We need to find time to get to the mall," he said. "I have to replace that gift for Lanie."

"What about Mom?" I asked.

He blinked at me. Then he shrugged. "Screw it. Let's tell her the truth. If we find him, she's gonna find out, anyway."

BACK AT THE house, we decided to let Mom lead the conversation. We started with how she was feeling.

As usual, her memory still came and went. But it was getting stronger. Now she knew why. And she remembered other things too: if I'd forgotten to give her a vitamin (and sometimes I did forget) she started feeling better. She would fight the fuzziness. In those times, she would call and email anyone who knew Dad. Something deep inside, something not even the drugs could destroy, had told her that the cops were wrong, that if Dad was alive, eventually, he'd come back. If not to her, than at least to a place that was familiar.

People didn't easily let go of their strongest and best memories. Something would draw him back and if she kept asking around, she'd find him. That was the hope.

I didn't question her logic on this. Nor did I remind her of all the memories she'd tossed to the wind. It seemed pointless and cruel.

Here is what Mom said when we told her that the police might have found Dad. The thing that shocked us all.

"I thought about going to Austin, too. We met at UT, remember? That's why he always wanted to go back there."

She didn't so much as bat an eyelash.

Truth? I didn't know whether to feel relieved or troubled. Had Dad wanted to go back to Austin? Had we just forgotten that in five years? What had he liked to do? Was he crazy about the UT Longhorns like Mr. Collins was about A&M? I remembered something about breakfast tacos—there was a place in Austin that he loved. Or was I just imagining it? For some reason, I pictured him saying the word "Taco" over and over again and laughing. *"Taco Taco Taco . . ."*

"Minor League Baseball in Round Rock," Mom told us in the heavy silence. "Your dad was a crazy person for minor league ball. He said it was purer than anything else these days."

"Oh," Casey said. "Huh."

I avoided my brother's eyes. We hadn't told her that part of Renfroe's confession. Nor had the police. Casey had convinced them that if Mom knew Dad had been so close, it would only make things worse.

Of course, it turned out I wasn't the only one who'd saved one of Dad's sports columns. Casey had one, too: the one he'd loaned Bryce to show to Zeke, the second photo, just to be sure.

Before Mom could add any more, Casey ran to his room to get the article. Together, the four of us read it and re-read it as we prepared to bring this thing to an end. And as we did, I knew they were all wondering the same thing I was: How clues to a person could sit there in plain sight without ever being seen.

If Dying Were Around the Corner
By MIKE SAMUELS

I have often written that I learned about baseball from my father. But this is not entirely true. I think mostly I learned about the game from the movies. We could argue endlessly about the best baseball movie: *Field of Dreams*, *The Babe Ruth Story*, *The Natural*, *Bull Durham*, *Pride of the Yankees* . . . the list is endless.

For me, it's *Bang the Drum Slowly*, a film from the 70's. Robert De Niro plays Bruce Pearson, a not-too-bright but big-hearted rookie catcher mentored by a veteran pitcher. When De Niro's character is diagnosed with Hodgkin's' disease, Henry Wiggen, big time pitcher, tries to help him through one more season of baseball.

It's a film about baseball, yeah. But mostly it's a film about life. All good sports movies are. Everyone knows that.

But baseball and by extension, baseball movies—they're a different breed. I think that this is because baseball is pure. Innocent. At least to me. It's life that sometimes sucks. Life that corrupts the inner core of that purity.

Bang the Drum Slowly is a story of courage and nobility and how those great qualities often come with tragedy. One of life's great ironies, I suppose— that too often we come to understand what's most important to us just as we find that we may not be around to enjoy it. Maybe that's why we love the glory of the sports fields, especially in the idealized form of the movies.

As Wiggen's character says in the film, "I don't know why you don't live it up all the time when dying is just around the corner, but you don't."

Which has always made me wonder: what if we really did live each day like we were dying? What exactly is it we would do?

For me, I think it would always include baseball (cont.)

THE COLUMN WENT on, but we stopped reading here. I think we all figured we'd learned as much as we were going to.

THE NEXT MORNING we headed out in Amber's Camaro, before five to beat the traffic. The Merc was at Lonnie's Body Shop. If we were going to keep it, we needed it worked on. I had no idea how we were going to pay for this. Not that the Merc was a particularly high priority.

Mom agreed to stay home, although she didn't want to. Her new doctor—who was hopefully not a crazy whack job—insisted. Dr. Kara Chang wanted Mom's system and chemical balance back in order. *Period*. She was totally humorless, like a cyborg. She wanted no trauma. She wanted no travel. Recovery might happen quickly; it might take a while. So Mom needed to stay put. Renfroe had confessed a lot, but as yet, he'd refused to divulge exactly what he'd mixed together in those fake vitamins. We were lucky that Amber's lab friend Terry had done his testing. Otherwise everyone might be even more flummoxed.

Secretly, I agreed Mom's staying put was for the best. I knew what it was like to get your hopes up about things that never happened. Mom wasn't strong enough for that yet. Still, I hated the way her eyes spilled over with tears when she waved good-bye to us. It was still dark out. It took all I had not to just drag her into the Camaro.

We stayed strong and stuck with the plan.

WE HIT AUSTIN a little before eight in the morning. I was starving.

"Are you serious?" My brother leaned forward from the back seat and poked at me. Amber had let me ride shotgun. "You know, just because you're hungry again doesn't mean you have to eat every five minutes."

"Making up for lost time," I told him. "Come on, let's just stop at that taco place up there." The sign read TACO TACO TACO. I guess they didn't want any confusion.

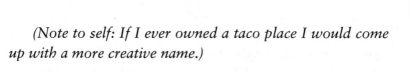

(Note to self: If I ever owned a taco place I would come up with a more creative name.)

ANYWAY, I NEEDED to fortify. We had a long day ahead of us. The lead Amber's cop friends had provided hadn't included an address. Our plan was to walk the campus at UT and any other place that Dad used to go. We would talk to people. Show them his picture. It was a long shot, but it was the best we could do. After that we'd head over to Round Rock. Baseball season was over, but we'd show his picture around. See what turned up. Mom's cell phone record had shown one call from an unknown number a few weeks back. She swore to us that it had been Dad.

Here is what I didn't say to Casey and definitely not to Amber:

What if Dr. Renfroe was telling the truth? Had Dad recovered his memories of us and still not come home? Things happen that we don't expect and don't understand. Like why people watch Dancing with the Stars, *or why my brother is now my guardian angel. I can accept that. I didn't know if I could accept a man who had remembered his life but not gone back to it.*

I will always believe that those thoughts were what caused what happened next. I had come to accept Maggie's philosophy of life. Things happen for a reason.

I shoved open the door to Taco Taco Taco, Amber and Casey walking behind me.

His back was to us at one of the little tables. He was eating something from a basket and sipping a mug of what smelled like really strong coffee. *Potato and egg*, I decided, still thinking about my breakfast. *Definitely guac on the side.*

When he turned around, time stood still. Just like it had

for a few crazy seconds in our squashed Prius when everything in my world went to hell and then to another place and then back to me. Just like it had when I'd tumbled through the open air of the Galleria atrium. My heart flew from my chest, whisked away in the morning breeze.

The man at the table was older than I remembered. His face had more lines. I had expected him to be thinner, but he was thicker, in all ways. Like everything that had happened had settled its weight on him.

I heard Amber clear her throat. She nudged me in the back.

"Go on," she said. "It's time."

Casey took my hand.

"Hey," said the man at the table. It was as though he was expecting us. Maybe in some way he was.

"Hey Dad," Casey and I said together. We crossed the space between us.

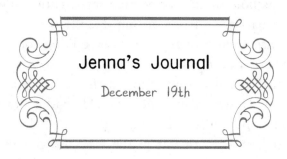

Jenna's Journal

December 19th

I wish I could write in this journal that after we found Dad in Taco Taco Taco (really, where else *could* we find him?) he came home with Casey and me and we all lived happily ever after. But our car accident had made that impossible, even if everything else had gone right. Which it did not.

"Did you leave us the Manny's gift certificate as a clue?" Casey asked him.

Dad looked at him blankly. He had no memory of it, and only the vaguest phantom sense of writing that final note to us, something he thought he had done while still in Houston. Just flashes were left: His hand holding a pen. A piece of paper. Someone (Dr. Renfroe he thought) telling him what to write. Maybe even saying "Good job," after he finished. Eventually we figured that Renfroe had left the Manny's gift certificate, either by accident or on purpose. He was after all, a conflicted crazy man with access to Dad's house keys. *Note to self: When we get home, we need to change the locks.*

"I started remembering about six months ago," Dad explained.

He was holding his coffee mug real tightly, almost like keeping a barrier in front of him. Finally we were getting to the truth, even though we'd been talking for over two hours. There'd been some brief hugging, too, at first. Brief and intense. I had never forgotten the feel of Dad's arms around me. That part was the same. He had a strong grip, like Casey's but different. And even though I knew that things might not work out in the ways I'd dreamed of, I knew when my father hugged me tight that he meant it. That he loved me. I just didn't know if that alone would be enough.

"I think once I knew how long I'd been gone," Dad said slowly, "it made it that much harder to come back. I don't expect you kids to understand. I just don't want you to hate me for it. I had no idea that I was that kind of man."

But it was more than that, I knew. It was the stuff he'd written about in those sports columns. The words that hinted that even if Renfroe hadn't screwed with our lives, being Mike Samuels might not have been enough. That was the part I couldn't accept quite yet. I knew that both Casey and I wanted him to say something in particular. Or a few things. That we were all he thought about. That Renfroe's scheme was so ass-backward that it *kept* him from coming home. That he didn't want to jeopardize our safety by showing his face. But he never did.

"I thought I was this big shot investigative reporter," Dad told us. "I'd hit it big for all of us if I tracked down this story. I didn't last five minutes. I put everyone in danger. I don't know how I could have been so stupid."

Amber stayed mostly quiet. She brought us our tacos

when they called our number. Then she said she had to duck outside to make a phone call. I'm sure she was just giving us our privacy.

My pulse started dancing when I took a bite of my potato and egg breakfast taco—extra guac, no cheese. It tasted like sawdust. I eyed my new Ariats suspiciously. Was this damn thing starting over again? Only this time with an EMT angel poisoning my boots? I nipped another tiny bite. Chewed carefully. Swallowed. Nope. Not poison. Just old-fashioned nerves. I blinked. Chomped a huge bite. This wasn't going to turn out good, but I was damned if I would let it ruin my love of breakfast tacos.

Once Amber was gone, Dad turned to Casey. "You look good, son. Real good. So, um, tell me about football. Bet you're still a superstar, huh?"

My heart jolted.

But Dad smiled. I realized he thought he was being nice. I blinked a few times, not wanting to cry again.

Casey met his gaze. "Had to quit," he said. He reached over his back and rubbed his shoulder blades, right where one of those wing nubs sat, hidden under shirt: the wings he'd spread wide when he flew to save me.

Dad looked surprised. Like he had not understood until just that moment that his absence meant anything more than lost years. Truth? He looked at Casey like he was seeing him for the first time.

"I took care of things while you were gone," Casey added. "I did the best I could."

I leaned across the table, eyeball to eyeball with our father. "Casey's been the man of the family. He's done a damn fine job."

OUR FATHER CAME back with us to Houston. But by then we were all clear that he wasn't coming home for good. Maybe things would work out one day, maybe not. He rode up front next to Casey. I was surprised that Amber let Casey drive, but she said that Casey and Dad needed father-son time. So Amber and I lounged in the back.

We only stopped once, at a kolache place on 290 that Amber knew. For someone who didn't have to eat, she had definitely kept up specific gastronomic habits.

"What is it with those things?" I asked as we waited to be rung up. "They're like crack to you or something."

Amber paid the checkout lady and peered outside to the parking lot, where Dad and Casey were huddled in intense conversation. "Sometimes. I just like to remember who I used to be," she said. "It isn't the big things you miss. It's the little ones. Red hawthorn berries that grew outside my house every fall. Bluebonnets in the spring. The smell of fresh kolaches hot from the oven."

I swallowed, wanting to make her feel better. "But you're still eating them. And you can still see the other stuff. It's not like they all disappeared."

"I know." Her eyes shimmered with a brief golden glow. "That's the point. As long as I'm here, like this, I get to have it. So I aim to have as much of it as I possibly can."

The white waxy sack of pastries sat between us the rest of the ride home.

MOM WAS AT the front door when we pulled up to our house. Her face lit up in the glow of the Gilroy's decorations. It was after nine and dark outside. For the first time it occurred to me that it was almost Christmas and we had done nothing about a tree.

My heart was pounding and my throat dried up. I was glad I hadn't snuck one of Amber's kolaches.

Dad climbed out of the car first. He stood there for a few long seconds. I could see Mom rocking back and forth like she was being torn between staying and running toward him. Casey solved the problem, of course.

"Hey," he shouted as he shoved the Camaro in park and swung out of the driver's seat. The door slammed. "We're here."

Dad walked slowly, then faster and faster up the walkway. He stopped in front of Mom. I kept holding my breath. Amber appeared next to me, the kolache bag clutched in her hand. Somehow this calmed me down. Was it the angel thing? Maybe just the kolaches. Like she'd told me: the little things.

Mom held her arms open. Dad spread his wide, too, and then they were hugging and holding each other and crying and he kissed her on the lips and then the cheeks and pressed his face to her neck, stroking her hair.

I wanted it to last forever. I wanted it to be like it was. *It could be*, I thought. *It would be. Why not?*

Then I thought about the column that Casey had showed me.

Did anyone really live like dying was around the corner? And why couldn't you do that right here at home?

I looked away from them. And saw that Amber's gaze was fixed on the edge of our yard, at a wild hawthorn tree we'd neglected to cut down. The whole yard had fallen apart when we'd forgotten how to live. Red berries were blooming in the darkness.

Jenna's Journal

January 12th

The night after we returned, Casey and Lanie went on that date they'd planned. He took her out for ice cream and then to the indoor skating rink that the mall folks set up every year from Thanksgiving through New Year's.

Mom had insisted that Lanie come to the house first. She couched it as "wanting to say hello." She remembered Lanie from before, she said. But I was more glad than annoyed. Mom was coming back.

The excruciating and awkward five minutes of small talk felt like five hours. Mostly Lanie talked about how nice it was to see me and Mom again. Her eyes flitted to Dad, but what could she say about him? He hadn't existed until now. "I like your outfit, Jenna," she added. I was wearing my new boots with a ruffled denim skirt and black sweater. Maggie and I were working on a signature look for me. If Lanie approved, then maybe this wasn't it.

I heard my father exhale a sigh of relief as Casey and Lanie left. Inwardly, I sighed, too, but probably not for the

same reasons. I watched out the window as my brother and
Lanie headed down the driveway. Casey reached one finger
under Lanie's chin. He pulled her close and kissed her. Their
lips stayed pressed together for a long time. The air around
them lit golden.

I still wanted to hate Lanie Phelps. Maybe I would even
be glad when the day came and Casey was gone and she was
the one who was dumped without warning.

Except I knew I wouldn't. Nobody deserved that.

RIGHT BEFORE NEW Year's Casey drove Dad back to Austin. We would see him once every couple of weeks. At least
that was the plan.

"I'll be freelancing for awhile," Dad told us. "*Houston
Chronicle* and *Austin Statesman*. Get my following back."
He said this firmly like he was confident it would happen. I
hoped that it would.

In between the sports-writing gigs, he'd work on his new
book—about the Minor League Baseball circuit.

"Might as well capitalize on where I've been," Dad said.
"You know. Lemonade out of lemons."

"Damn lot of lemonade," my brother observed.

I'd have commented that he was being sour about things,
but I figured the joke would fall flat. Instead I said, "If you
ever do a sequel to the barbeque book, I'm your girl." By
then we'd all agreed that it would be best if he abandon the
Tex Mex restaurant guide idea. Manny's, by the way, had
closed down indefinitely. Amber had mentioned that Terry
had told her that the government had taken over the investigation from the cops, looking into whether Manny had
managed to sell Renfroe's drug to anyone who was a true
world threat.

fake lamb's wool lining, a gift from Casey. Honestly? I looked pretty fine.

I guess Ryan Sloboda thought so, too, because there he was at my elbow when I ambled out of Ima Hogg into the cool January air. "Love the lining," he commented. He flicked a finger over the fake lamb's wool stuff.

Ryan's braces had come off over vacation. They'd definitely done the trick with that pesky overbite, but he was still pretty awkward about socializing.

"Thanks," I said. I was pretty awkward about it all, too. My brother was not exactly a role model in this regard. BAI (Before Angel Incident), he'd been too stoned to care most days. AAI (After Angel Incident) he was suddenly visible to females again. Not that he noticed. He had eyes only for Lanie. Now that they were an official couple, they spent lots of time doing annoying official couple things, like making out in the backseat of the Merc. Better than the laptop shenanigans at least.

Ryan was still hovering in my personal space. He smelled like oranges and sweat and possibly the burrito he had eaten at lunch. Not as bad a combination as you'd think.

"Um," he said. "You going to the basketball game later?"

I had a feeling that more was going on here, but neither of us were quite sure how to get to it. Two possibilities were blinking in my brain: Run. And I wonder if his lips taste like oranges.

"Jenna Samuels!" My brother's voice rang out from the car line. "Ain't got all day. Get a move on."

I frowned. Ryan backpedaled a few steps. The distance let me notice his hair, which was spiked up just a little. I found myself wondering what those spikes would feel like if I ran my fingers over them.

"Jenna!" Casey bellowed again.

There was an uncomfortable moment where Dad s
gested the possibility of a tell-all book about what had h;
pened to our family.

"You really want people knowing you're not living wi
us now?" Casey asked.

"But that's part of the fall out," my father said.

Casey frowned. A few beats later, Dad dropped the idea.

ABOUT A WEEK after Dad returned to his new home,
Texas Children's Hospital called, offering Mom a part-time
gig as an in-house speech therapist. Amber had gotten her
the interview. I was still not sure what to make of Amber
Velasco. Would she ever tell me the rest of her story? Had
she told Casey? Somehow, I suspected he knew. But right
now he was in the happy bubble with Lanie. I decided not
to press him.

"I'm so nervous," Mom said the morning she was due to
start. "What if I'm not good at this anymore?"

I gave her my best "you can do it" look. "It'll be like falling off a log," I said. "Just watch out for doctors with too
much chest hair and poison vitamins."

"Bad joke, sweetie," she said.

"Agreed," I acknowledged.

THAT SAME AFTERNOON, Casey was waiting for me
when I got out of school. This was a surprise. I had started
taking the school bus home in the afternoons again on
the days Maggie's mom wasn't available to give us rides.
I was wearing my Ariats and a pair of black jeans that
Mom had bought me for Christmas (her first step toward
New Mom Normal; she'd gone with Casey to the mall),
a scoop neck gray tee, and a new red hoodie with fuzzy

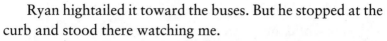

Ryan hightailed it toward the buses. But he stopped at the curb and stood there watching me.

I stomped over to the Merc. Amber—in jeans and a sweater, not her EMT outfit—was riding shotgun. Must be her day off.

"Get in," Casey directed me. "And stay away from football players. They're trouble." (The day before, Casey had expressed interest in trying out for football again, a plan that Amber described as "reckless and imprudent," two of my new favorite words. Look them up!)

"You are a mental case," I told my brother. I waved to Ryan, taking my time about it, then slid into the backseat. "Don't you have anything better to do?"

"He does, actually," Amber said.

"What do you mean? What's going on?"

"Jenna," Amber replied, "don't you think it's weird that the cops bought my stupid stunt-diving story without even bothering to question it? And now there's this whole huge global case that the government has taken over?"

Yes. It was weird. But this was not how I wanted to learn that my brother had more to do than just protect me from bad stuff, or at least from Ryan Sloboda's lame attempt at romance. Of course, two seconds later I saw Casey's gaze lock onto the shapely butt of Cammie Northrup's older sister. Guess he was scouting a backup plan in case the whole Lanie romance fizzled. Unlikely, of course: at least until Lanie discovered that my brother's angel pheromones had bamboozled her into that backseat with him.

"Someone up there likes me," Casey said with a cocky-looking grin.

Angel Test Question #6: Is the A-word acting like an egotistical jerk?

Check. I didn't want to smile back, but I did.

"The world might need him," Amber persisted. "I'm serious."

"Then the world," I told Amber Velasco and my brother, "is totally screwed."

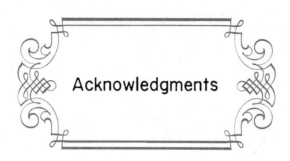

Acknowledgments

Jen Rofe, for butt-kicking, boot-stomping, and insisting that I can get it right. Also for the occasional therapeutic cocktail or two when I'm in LA.

Daniel Ehrenhaft, for knowing what I mean even before I figure it out myself, and for patience and insight and thinking I'm funny. In a good way. This one goes to eleven.

Rick, Jake, and Kellie, for ignoring me when I'm whiny and obsessive and for making me laugh and laugh and laugh.

Critique partners, fellow writers—including but not limited to my retreat buddies from the Lodge of Death— for walking the walk with me and building the craft. You are my village.

To the rest of you—consider yourself thanked.